PRISNMS

ALSO BY GARTH ST OMER

Syrop
A Room on the Hill
Shades of Grey
Nor Any ountry
J—, Black Bam and the Masqueraders

GARTH ST OMER

PRISNMS

PEEPAL TREE

First published in Great Britain in 2015
Peepal Tree Press Ltd
17 King's Avenue
Leeds LS6 1QS
England

ISBN13: 9781845232429

Supported using public funding by
ARTS COUNCIL
ENGLAND

PART ONE

CHAPTER ONE

The noise I had been hearing in my sleep became, abruptly as I awoke, the ringing of the telephone. I reached eagerly for it. But it was not Peggy calling from California to say she was returning from her vacation. It was Selwyn calling from Texas. Red was dead, he said, shot in the head during a card game. I said nothing. But, after thirty years, the light burst on suddenly again in the nightclub basement filled with empty cartons and the smell of stale liquor and, even before I could disengage from C.B.'s sister, I heard his drunken, "I'll kill you, you son of a bitch," and felt the excruciating pain, as blinding as the sudden light, where he hit me on the arm I had instinctively raised for protection. My arm hanging limply at my side, my mind splintered into brilliant bits of pain, fear and incomprehension, I was backing away from him even as he raised the iron bar to hit me again. From behind the old ping-pong table which I managed to keep between C.B. and myself, I heard for the first time Beatrice's screams. Then Paul and Selwyn were in the room and Selwyn was holding C.B. against him from behind with one of his weightlifter's arms and wrenching the iron bar from him with the other, while C.B. shouted, "Leave me alone. I'll kill that son of a bitch, that traitor, that mother-fucking double-crosser."

My arm, holding the telephone, seemed to ache now as much as it did when C.B. had broken it. And as I listened to the details of Red's sordid death in an American ghetto, I thought how lucky I was that C.B. – not yet become Red and, until that moment, my best friend – had been no karate expert when he attacked me. For, on that small island in the Caribbean where we then lived I did not have a gun, as his killer had, to shoot him dead with. I heard Selwyn elaborate on Red's murder but I wasn't listening to him. I was thinking of Beatrice.

Several years after her brother had broken my arm, and I was back on the island recovering from the automobile accident that had almost killed me in London where I was a medical student, she told me what C.B. had said to her at home that night – that she had finally fucked his best friend just as she had fucked every other man on the island and all that was left for her to do now was to fuck him, her own brother. She and I were sitting on the veranda of her home above her hairdressing salon, after work. Below us, the Roman Catholics were going to Benediction in the cathedral across the street. Beatrice was waiting for it to be dark so she could meet with her lover. She was happy, she said. Life had been good. Her hairdressing business was prospering. She was building a house ("a huge house, like everyone else these days") in the suburbs. And now, after all those years, she was going to have a child. She patted her swollen belly which, up to that moment, both herself and I had not commented on. She knocked on wood. The town, she said, was gossiping about her more than ever. Her eyes lit up mischievously. This time they wanted to know who the father of the child was. I thought I had never seen her look more beautiful. I felt the completeness with which she had broken away from the past in which I had left her mired seven years before. I felt she had a new sense of herself, her independence, her freedom from the opinion of others. I was glad she could not have known, looking at my noncommittal face, how ashamed she made me feel of the younger man I was who had abandoned her.

On the telephone, Selwyn was telling me of the arrangements he had made for the funeral. He would fly in from Texas the day after tomorrow to attend it. He couldn't stay. He had to return soon afterwards. "I'm a working man," he said. "You know that. Not like you and Paul."

I said, "I'll tell Paul."

"He knows. I called him first," Selwyn said. "At least he's not out of the country. He'll be able to attend."

He hung up. I lay in the dark, my eyes closed, intensely awake.

I had not defended Beatrice. I had joined the rest of the small town in condemning her. Listening to all the rumours, I told myself that I despised her for what I heard she had become. In the end, I persuaded myself that I, too, could make her open her legs. And as if enslaved by her new habit and utterly submissive to her new reputation, unaware of my pain or of my unexamined contempt for her, she had laughed mirthlessly and not resisted when I led her from the dance floor. Then, standing with her against the dirty wall of the nightclub basement, her dress pulled up above her waist, I was angrily, inexpertly, trying to imitate all those who boasted what they had done to her, when the lights came on and her brother, my best friend, almost killed me.

But, during that strange period of our reunion on the island, while my breast healed following my motor accident in England, and I watched her getting happily bigger and bigger with another man's child, and endured her constant happy talk about its father, the married Roman Catholic whom she said she loved, Beatrice did more than complete my shame and rekindle my admiration.

One evening, waiting with me as usual on the verandah for it to be dark , she told me she had been raped. She spoke of herself as of a character in a book that we had both read. She told me when, where, and how. She told me by whom. She smiled as though she had forgiven the very respectable man whose name she mentioned.

I could hardly bear listening to her.

But, for the first time, I understood her brother's rage. C.B. had wanted to expose the influential man who had violated his sister, something, Beatrice said, their mother had forbidden him to do. "She preferred to avoid embarrassment for ourselves and for the small Protestant community to which we belonged. She wanted to keep the matter secret. As if," she added, "the whole town was not already talking about it."

This was not true. I was hearing about Beatrice's rape for the first time. The sickening rumours I had at first refused to believe, then had angrily tried to respond to in the nightclub basement, were not about Beatrice being raped, but about how easy it had suddenly become for men, all men, every sort of man, to sleep with her. On the veranda, waiting impatiently for it to be dark, Beatrice laughed.

"You must remember I was, like you, only sixteen. No wonder I thought I'd never feel clean again! Of course, he would never have dared if Daddy were still alive. But by then we were defenceless. We had become dependent and vulnerable. You know our story."

We all knew it. Her father had falsified the books in the important firm where he was an accountant and been permitted to resign. When he died soon afterwards, the small Protestant community, preoccupied with keeping up appearances on the largely Roman Catholic island, rallied to help the family. It could not stop the rumours about Mr Wilson's suicide. But it found Mrs Wilson a job for which she was not qualified but which paid her well; and it raised money to help the family maintain its social position on the island.

At the head of the salvaging was the respectable man who had raped her!

"He helped us a lot," Beatrice said. "We never had to give up our servants. Mamma, God bless her soul, did not want to be ungrateful. She felt indebted. I understood. But not C.B. He never did. You remember!"

I remembered only too well. Confused and angered by the rumours about Beatrice who had not yet dropped out of school and, in her blue-and-white convent uniform, seemed to me as lovely and as unapproachable as ever, I had withdrawn into my private contemplation of what was so inexplicably happening to her and, though no one else knew it, to me. I did not know that C.B. quarrelled constantly with his mother or raged impotently at home about hypocrisy and "double standards" and a solidarity he qualified as criminal. C.B., Beatrice explained, had promised his mother not to discuss the matter in public and had kept his promise. I knew only that he seemed suddenly to have become contemptuous of all that our small Protestant community had required us to do. He ceased to perform well as a student at the Catholic college, the only boys' secondary school on the island. He smoked and drank in public. He consorted openly with Roman Catholic women. He publicly frequented prostitutes. I often wanted, but had not dared, to be as rebellious as he was. But C.B., the angry, impotent rebel and I, the angry and confused newcomer, less than a year and a half on the island where my father had come to be a magistrate, became close friends. After he broke my arm, our community made it possible, by their subscriptions, for him to go to his uncle in America. After he left the island, I never set eyes on C.B. again.

But I heard of him.

In London, where I was a medical student, I heard that C.B., become Red because of his reddish brown hair and yellowish complexion, a holder of karate championships, had, in a deep rage, killed an unarmed man in a fight. Later, I heard he was involved with narcotics. He was always in and out of jail. Safe in England, as I then thought I was, secure in my achievement, and virtually engaged to Sarah, the daughter of an English peer, I felt that Red was someone I had never known and did not want ever to meet. Beatrice, on the island, had heard the stories, too. C B., she said, had soon stopped answering her letters, which were returned unopened. She stopped writing. She wiped a tear from her face. It was the only time while I waited with her on the veranda that I saw her unhappy.

But it was not this image of Beatrice saddened about her brother that I took back to England. It was the image of Beatrice preparing to give birth to a child that I wished had been my own, and so radiantly happy that I dared not tell her that I loved and admired her now as deeply as I had once imagined I had done during those early years when she was unaware of my teenage passion.

After six months of convalescence, though the rent in my sternum was not yet fully mended, I said goodbye to her and returned to my medical studies. I threw myself into my life in London with Sarah and Ekua, as if there were no other place in which I had a past or to which I ever expected to return. When the time came for me to choose between the two women, neither of whom I loved and yet neither of whom I could afford to lose, between the not-yet-pregnant, aristocratic medical student and the pregnant ex-student nurse from Africa, now without a job and living alone in her one-room apartment, the choice was not difficult.

I had discussed marriage with both. Sarah put it off somewhere in the future, after our graduation. But Ekua, happily pregnant, behaved as if her marriage to me was inevitable, and it had to take place before we left together for

Africa. She read to me from her father's latest letter. She had already been dismissed by the hospital and we had just made love. The single bed sagged beneath our weight and that of our unborn child. Under the sheets, her naked body was warm against my own. Her father thought that she and I were married. He called me his son-in-law. He was waiting eagerly to meet me.

I was about to graduate. My professors were predicting great things for me. It seemed that I need never know again the uncertainty about the future that my father, by his death, had exposed me and my mother to. But his sudden death, after he had struggled so hard and for so long to succeed, had shown me that nothing that had not already happened was certain, and that the future, no matter how well-planned it was or how brilliant it seemed, was not immune to accident. I knew accident. I had recovered from one. I wanted to avoid accident. I wanted my children to be safer than I had been. Africa, it seemed to me, could not guarantee my children's safety. And in England, which I considered my home and where I intended to spend the rest of my life, Ekua, tropical transplant like myself, could not have been expected to provide it. Sarah and her inheritance could. And so, one night, soon after Ekua had read me her father's letter, I put on the perforated condom I had ready in my wallet and made love to Sarah.

I wanted a quiet wedding. There was no need to let Ekua know that Sarah and I were getting married. But Sarah had endured much for my sake and wanted to avoid any semblance of scandal. We had to marry at once and our wedding had to appear as normal as possible. It was an elaborate affair, full of her relatives and friends. And photographers! I was calm and resigned the next day when I saw a picture of myself in the *Times*, dressed in tails and morning coat, standing happily next to my new wife. I was only a little surprised, two or three nights later, as Sarah and I were returning home to the house just outside London that her parents had given her, when I saw Ekua emerge onto the drive and stand, big with my child, in the headlight's of Sarah's car. Her face was bathed with tears.

Sarah exclaimed and stepped suddenly on the brake. I jumped out of the car and moved quickly to Ekua. In a loud voice, I asked her kindly, as kindly as I could, who she was and where she had come from. I heard the car door open. I began to wink furiously at Ekua and, in the same loud voice, asked Ekua whether she was lost.

She did not answer. Big with my child, bearing it low within her beautifully angular body, she stood in the glare of the headlights and looked at me. Then, slowly, she moved past Sarah and myself and headed for the road leading back to London.

"Do you know her?" Sarah asked.

I told her with a straight face that I had never seen Ekua before. And, as she disappeared into the night, I shouted that if she were lost and told me where she lived I would be happy to take her home. I had wanted, but not dared, to touch her.

Sarah said, "That's very strange. Who do you suppose she is? Is there anything we can do?"

I shrugged. "It doesn't seem so, does it?"

I never saw Ekua again. And as days, then weeks, then months passed and I heard and saw nothing of her, I felt more and more relieved, safer and safer. When Richard was born, my contentment and sense of achievement knew no bounds. I congratulated myself. I had chosen well. Ekua, so discreet the night she had emerged onto our drive, would do nothing, I was sure, to disturb my contentment.

One day, I came home from the hospital where I was a

resident and saw my son asleep, as usual, in his crib before the bay window and his mother, my wife, asleep beside him. I bent over and, as I sometimes did when she was asleep, placed my lips lightly on hers to wake her. She opened her eyes, looked sleepily for a moment at me, then spat in my smiling face and handed me Ekua's letter with the photograph of Ekua and myself, and a photograph of our son, alone.

Our divorce, unlike our wedding, was quick, quiet and unpublicized. It was not yet finalized when Sarah forwarded to me the letter from Ekua's lawyer. There was no photograph this time, only information. The child was a boy. (I had known that.) Its name was my own. (I hadn't.)

It was born etc. etc. If I wished, I could communicate with mother and with child through the writer of the letter. I went to his chambers. He was an African practising in London. He confirmed that Ekua was his client. Was she in London? He couldn't answer that. Was she in England, then? He couldn't answer that. Back in Africa? He had no comment. His professional reserve did not conceal his disdain. I left him, and decided it was time, too, for me to leave England.

I had always intended, after I had practised for two or three years, to specialize in gynaecology. So, now, I applied to medical schools in Canada and the United States. When an Ivy League University offered me more money than I had ever imagined I might receive for a fellowship, if I agreed to study psychiatry, I abandoned the idea of studying gynaecology and headed to America, somewhat warily, to become a psychiatrist. I told myself I would remain in America only for as long as I had to. I would be careful. Circumspect. Unlike in England, I would live in America as if there were another country that I loved and to which I was impatient to return.

CHAPTER TWO

At first, I was careful. I kept to myself and only accepted the invitations the university gave to all its foreign students. Personal invitations of the sort I had been delighted to receive and eager to accept in England, where I felt I was beginning a new life, I now steadfastly refused.

I did join a study group with three American classmates – Jonathan, Reginald and Porter. We lived on the same floor of the university-owned building and studied together in one another's apartments, in rotation, three times a week. Jonathan was a graduate of Columbia, and Reginald and Porter had roomed together at Harvard, so I knew I could only benefit from working with them. But, outside of those working sessions, I tried to have as little as possible to do with any of my new colleagues.

One day, about a month after I had been in America, as I walked among the crowd outside the University, a man stopped so suddenly in front of me that I could not avoid running into him. I said "Sorry" and tried to move on. He moved too, and blocked my way again. I thought he had inadvertently moved in front of me, looked briefly up at his face, smiled and tried to continue. I thought he looked familiar. Once more he placed himself in front of me; this time I looked closely at him, still unwilling to acknowledge Selwyn behind the elegant three-piece suit, the unfamiliar moustache and full, well-trimmed beard. But I recognized his low chuckle, and when I mentioned his name as if asking a question I feared he might correctly answer, he burst out in the old laugh I remembered.

He led me to a bar across the street. He ordered whiskey for himself.

"Top shelf," he said. Nothing less would do for the occasion. Sipping my beer, I tried to seem as enthusiastic about our meeting as he was. In England, I had stopped answering the letters he had written me from Aruba where he had gone to work in the oil refineries. I had not heard from him in years! Nor had I expected ever to see him again. Now, sitting at the table opposite to him, I was surprised and confused by the elegant reproduction of the mediocre student, powerful weigh-lifter and excellent athlete who had saved my life.

"Boy," he said. "You could've knocked me down with a feather." He laughed. "You think you ever going back?"

"Perhaps," I said.

But returning to live on the island was the last thing I wanted to do.

"At least you're honest," he said. "You not like Paul. You don't say home, home, home all the time and still continue to live here. He doesn't really live here. He says he does, but he's always out of the country, always somewhere else, on tour somewhere in Australia, Japan, South America – you name it. He own property all over the place but not an inch on the island. But he's always talking about home, home, home." He paused. "You know about the sheep farm in New Zealand?"

I knew.

"And you know where he is now?"

"In Brazil," I said, "he'll be performing a series of concerts in South America."

"Right. That's how he does live. He doesn't live here, in America. He living everywhere. The whole world is his home. As for me," Selwyn tapped the table top decisively with his finger, "my home is right here. Nobody making me go back."

He chuckled. "Cockroaches, centipedes. Chicken backs and necks. And DDT! But nobody going to dump on me again. I'll do the dumping now."

He pulled out his wallet and showed me a card. He said proudly, "I'm an American citizen. I'm making a very good living."

He worked in a chemical factory, spoke casually of accidental near-releases of lethal gases, and of pressure locks, valves and fail-safe devices. The work sounded dangerous, but he was obviously very satisfied with his life. He spoke proudly of Pat, his wife from another Caribbean island, and of Cheryll and Helen, his teenage daughters, both in college.

"I couldn't do that if I didn't come here," he said. "Thank God for America! Look, finish your drink. I want to show you something."

He had hardly touched his. As we stood up to leave, I asked, "Still working out?"

He chuckled and didn't answer. But he seemed to push his chest out and to hold himself more erect.

He drove past the city's Cultural Center. It was full of tourists and sightseers.

"Cheryll, my daughter, works there. She's a tour guide. She can give you a free tour anytime you like. Paul got her the job." He chuckled. "After all, isn't that what friends are for?"

Later, he double-parked in front of an apartment building a few blocks away. He pointed with his chin to the uniformed doorman standing just within the revolving glass door and to the uniformed, armed man next to him.

"You see how they watching us? Heh, heh. Just try to get in there! The place like a damn fortress. They want to know what your grandfather's brother's concubine name is. Then, when you tell them, they have to call upstairs. And while you waiting to hear what they does have to say, they watching you like a hawk. That's where Paul does stay when he's in town. That's why he'll never marry. With all this, who needs a wife to take care of him, eh? Look, look! You see how they watching us? They getting nervous. He getting ready to shoot."

The two men were paying no attention to us. Selwyn drove off. He said, "Now, I'll take you to another place. Tell me if you recognize it."

Ten minutes later, he asked me, "You know where you are?"

I knew! The people I looked at on the street were like people I had grown up with and lived almost half of my life among. I should have felt at home here. But the university's foreign- student advisor had told us how dangerous the area behind the university was. She called it a neighbourhood. She had not used the word ghetto. I felt that I was in alien, dangerous territory.

"Red's Kingdom!" Selwyn said, laughing.

We were stopped at a red light. He tapped the steering wheel with his fingers. Then he became uncharacteristically silent and looked straight ahead.

"You better lock your door. Just in case. You never know."

I did.

Selwyn said, "Look out!" and ducked.

I ducked. Selwyn came up chuckling. I sat up. After all those years, I had allowed him to play another trick on me!

I smiled sheepishly. The light turned green. He moved the car smoothly forward.

I asked, "Do you come here often?"

He laughed. "No man. I only wanted to show you Red's territory."

He never offered to take me into the ghetto again. He wanted, he said, to introduce me to the real city, to take me, in his words, "on the town", to show me the nightclubs where the men were required to wear suits and where he entertained his "not-yet-Americanized women from Europe". I became accustomed to his telephone calls, but often, citing work, I would find reasons not to accept his invitations to go out with him.

Determined to be careful and circumspect, envious of his confident ease and assumption of freedom in an America that I distrusted and feared, but had allowed myself to be lured to, I made Selwyn my surrogate, a modern knight errant in black face and a three-piece suit, happily coursing his way in his automobile through America's streets, to and from its motels with his women, the popular music coming in a steady stream from the car's four speakers, its windows up, in all seasons, no matter how cold or hot it was outside, and he enclosed comfortably within it, as if in a bubble that would never burst. His phallus was his lance, and I his fearful, repressed and not always believing – yet not wholly unadmiring – squire.

And it was, in part, because of him, that I took the first step of the journey that would lead me to the cafeteria in the park, and, from there, out into the rain to Carol, the American woman who would become my wife.

CHAPTER THREE

I had not gone to the cafeteria to meet Carol. I went to meet Janice whom I had spoken to on the telephone when I was looking for a bank to deposit some money in. I had chosen one closer to the university than the one where she worked, but I called every now and then to exchange a word or two with her. That first time she complimented me on my accent. "So English," she said, "so cultured."

She was not the only one in America who made me aware of how I spoke. I had begun to notice a peculiar look of recognition, which I found insolent in its familiarity, directed at me by people who I was sure had never before seen me. Once these strangers heard me speak, they seemed surprised. They remarked on my accent. They asked where I had come from and what I had come to America to do. They became curious and almost friendly. But no matter how friendly these strangers became, I never ceased to feel that my accent had, in some way, enabled me to escape from them.

On the telephone with Janice, it was otherwise. She was neither surprised by the way I spoke nor curious about who I was or where I had come from. I never felt that I had escaped from her. My conversations with her became more comfortable than my ever more infrequent telephone conversations with Selwyn. Janice, in time, became like an old friend. We had never met, but not even with my study group colleagues had I been as comfortable with an American as I was speaking to her.

And yet, my study group colleagues were very friendly. Their frequent social invitations – when I wanted only to be left alone – made me feel I was the foreign guest to whom each was determined to play gracious American host. I was flattered that Porter constantly invited me to his family's estate home in the hills, a day's drive from the city; that Jonathan should take me to a service in his Reform temple and, afterwards, to his parents' apartment where he produced his unpublished novel manuscripts and asked me to say nothing about them to the others; and that Reginald should invite me to his mother's home in the ghetto, the place Selwyn called Red's kingdom, and ask me, again and again, until he grew tired of my refusals and stopped, to go there once a week to teach in his old high school with him.

These invitations were distractions. In America, unlike in England, I wanted only to be left alone. But Jonathan, Porter and Reginald were excellent colleagues whom it was most advantageous to have as working partners, and I did not want to seem rude or unsociable to them. I was also finding it more and more difficult to suppress the friendliness and camaraderie that I felt developing naturally between my colleagues and myself. Increasingly, I felt guilty for wanting to be no more than a colleague to each of them. I discovered, though, that Porter had never invited Jonathan or Reginald to his estate home, and that it was I alone, and never Jonathan or Porter, whom Reginald invited to go into the ghetto. But even when I began to feel naive and duped because of what I discovered about the asocial and segmented relationships my colleagues maintained with each other (such as, I have to admit, I wished to maintain with them), I found it difficult not to feel flattered by their attention and their repeated demonstrations of friendship. I told myself that it was natural for each of them to want to introduce and initiate me, the ignorant foreigner, into his personal experience as an American. I allowed each flattering invitation from them, each friendly telephone conversation with Janice, each more-and-more-unwilling excursion into the city with Selwyn, to lead me, a little farther each time, away from the fearful America that its history and recent events had created in my imagination.

Each offered journey became another tentative, exploratory reaching out beyond the restricting frontiers of my imagined America, taking me a little farther into its wilderness. Whether the next call from Janice, the next excursion with Selwyn into the not-anymore-so-alien city, the next flattering invitation from my study group colleagues, they prepared and made possible – as into territory reconnoitred, cleared and presumed safe – my subsequent, careful advance into the actual America in which I was living so circumspectly.

My invitation to Janice to have lunch with me in the park, made on an impulse one day, because I had begun to wonder what she looked like, was an act born of this new confidence. I had begun to feel that the America I distrusted and feared, but had allowed myself to be lured to, might yet be safe.

Janice responded enthusiastically to my invitation.

"I was beginning to think we would never meet," she said. She would be dressed in a taupe pant-suit. I asked her what colour taupe was. She laughed. "Don't you know?" Then, "I'll make it even easier for you. I'll wear a flower in my hair. An anemone." There was the usual laughter and something, which I took to be excitement, in her voice. I did not tell her I did not know what an anemone was. I looked it up.

When I entered the cafeteria, I made her out at once, sitting at a table with another woman and expectantly facing the entrance. I thought, "So that's what taupe is!" smiled and waved. Janice's eyes flitted over me. She seemed not to recognize the brown suit, the brown-and-white striped tie and the tan raincoat I had described to her. But I knew what an anemone was. I walked towards it confidently, the smile still on my face. Janice, the flower in her hair, the tip of her brownish-grey pant-suit showing above the table, continued to look expectantly at the entrance, speaking all the while to her friend, as if the man I had carefully described had not just entered the room. I walked past her and her expectant smile, and sat at a table behind her. I recalled her voice as intimately as if I were still listening to it on the telephone.

"It feels strange to have to describe myself to you after all this time. I feel I have known you forever," she had said.

And, after I had described myself: "I'm sure not to miss you, now."

A waitress, red-haired and smiling, pencil and pad ready, came to take my order. I asked for coffee and a tuna sandwich. I wanted to disguise my accent so as not to reveal myself to Janice, but, when I spoke, my voice was raised, not pleasantly. I had tried in vain to control it. The waitress stepped backwards. Her smile disappeared. I wished to reassure her. I heard myself begin to say in the accent Janice said she admired, "Excuse me…" and stopped speaking. The waitress was looking at me curiously.

I smiled at her. I said, in an accent I intended to be American, "Excuse me. I didn't mean to frighten you."

The waitress laughed good-naturedly. She came closer and patted my shoulder. She said, "You'll soon get the hang of it, sir. Did you say a cup of coffee and a tuna sandwich?"

I nodded. She left.

Through the glass wall of the cafeteria I could see people walking in bright sunshine in the park. I was embarrassed that the waitress had laughed at my attempt to sound like an American and had felt it necessary to comfort me. In London, Sarah had not allowed me to try my new English accent in public until she was sure I spoke it like one who had always used it. The effect had been startling. It was as if I had been instantaneously transformed into an Englishman of the class to which she belonged.

Now I heard Janice say, "Do you think he'll come?"

She was still waiting for the Englishman who had described himself to her.

The waitress appeared with my coffee and sandwich, and my bill. I smiled at her as warmly as I could. I wanted to let her know that I had not meant to frighten her, but I did not trust thyself to speak. She said, "I hope that makes you feel better, sir."

I nodded. She smiled once more and walked away. I heard Janice say, "I wonder why he isn't here. It's nearly one."

I looked at the anemone in her hair and at the pant-suit whose colour I learned was taupe and sipped my coffee and ate my tuna fish sandwich – I had learned to enjoy tuna fish sandwiches – and watched the people walking in the park.

Then, abruptly, as had been happening during the last few days of November, the weather changed. The sky darkened. The wind began to blow violently. The cafeteria, lit up a moment before by the light of the bright sunshine coming through its glass walls, darkened, too. Almost immediately, it began to rain. The room filled rapidly with people.

I heard Janice say, "He's not going to come now, for sure. I wonder what could have happened."

She sounded disappointed.

Lit only dimly now by discreet electric lights, the cafeteria hummed with the low murmur of many people speaking pleasantly to one another. The tables, mine included, were all soon occupied, the aisles full of people. The air, as in the pubs Sarah and I had frequented, was beginning to be tinged with the smell of cigarette smoke. I had learned to like that smell. I had thought of it as socially reassuring – all those people, of the same class, surrounded by cigarette smoke, talking and laughing and having a good time.

I could no longer hear Janice's voice. I got up from the table at which three members of a group of four had joined me, offered my seat to the fourth who was standing nearby and made my way to the nearest glass wall to watch the rain, which I heard falling heavily now on the roof. But the glass wall was rapidly filming over, and, soon, I could only hear it.

One summer, while Sarah was on the continent with her parents, Ekua and I had gone to spend a few hours in the countryside outside London. But the day, splendid when we started out, soon turned to a persistent drizzly rain that caught us in open fields just outside the village, and we returned wet and uncomfortable in a grey afternoon to the empty train station. We waited a long time for our train. Once, turning from the far end of the platform to which I had walked, I saw Ekua standing where I had left her, her back to me, her hands in her coat pockets, looking at the tracks along which our train should come. Her shoulders were hunched the way shoulders are hunched when pockets are not deep enough for the hands we push into them. She had already lost her job. But she was happy. We were going to be married. We would be going back together to Africa. Paul's letter from Strasbourg was in my pocket. He could not attend Sarah's and my wedding. He asked me what would happen to Ekua and her unborn child and wondered what I would say to Sarah's children about their maternal grandparents. I had told him of their objections to their daughter's marriage to me.

When I came up to Ekua, I placed a hand gently on her shoulder. She put her hand on mine and turned to smile at me, as though the rain had not turned a promising day into a disaster, and she and I were merely waiting to return from an enjoyable picnic.

The train we waited for never came. There had been an accident. It would be a long time before the next train. Ekua and I walked from the station in a heavy drizzle to a pub in the village. The air inside the pub, as it had become now in the cafeteria, was blue with cigarette smoke. Ekua's eyes began to water. She seemed, as she actually had been when I last saw her, to be crying.

The glass wall of the cafeteria was white now with vapour. Behind me, the room was full of the comforting sound of human beings talking pleasantly to one another. Idly, I wiped off some of the moisture from the wall with a paper napkin. In the rain and wind, I saw a woman, her uncovered hair high in an Afro above her head, playing with an obviously delighted child. The sight of the woman and child in the pouring rain was so unexpected that I turned and looked behind me, as if I feared there might be someone to ask me why they were out in the rain by themselves.

But no one else had seen them. No one in the cafeteria had seen me spring back, startled, from the wall. I went up to the wall again and, with my napkin, wiped away some more of the steam on it. Water was streaming down its outer side, and the images of the woman and her child wavered, were indistinct and sometimes disappeared completely behind a sudden, more heavy flow of water. I strained to cling visually to them. And when the woman straightened up and put her hands in the pockets of her coat and hunched her shoulders, as though the pockets were not deep enough to contain her hands, I turned abruptly from the wall and walked out of the cafeteria and into the rain towards the woman whom I would later know as Carol, who would become my wife.

I had started out towards her spurred by a painful memory and by my sudden feeling of aloneness in the crowded cafeteria. But, in the wind and the rain, my face tingling after the warmth inside, I gave myself up wholly to the anger that Janice had generated. I imagined that she was looking at me through the space I had cleared on the wall of the cafeteria, and defiantly I postured for her. I became tribesman and fellow warrior to two people I had never seen before. I thought mother and child splendidly rebellious out in the rain by themselves. I felt angrily splendid and rebellious, too, as I walked in the rain towards them. I opened my shoulders, straightened my spine, lengthened my stride. I strode confidently towards Carol as though she was waiting for me.

She must not have seen me approach for she jumped almost out of her skin when I said, "Sister!" to her. She turned. Beneath her open raincoat, I saw the wet cloth of her dress sticking to her breasts and to her slightly rounded stomach. Her hips were wide. Like Sarah's. I felt quickened, as though she had just opened a dam of sexual desire, fed by the memories of Sarah and Ekua, which until then I had suppressed, and fed now, too, as she stared at me, by the promise that her body had just made to me.

She turned and walked away. I followed her at a distance, because I did not want to frighten her. I raised my voice above the wind and the rain.

"Sister!"

She turned sharply, angrily, to face me. I stopped where I was. I could hardly see her face through the slanting, driven lines of rain. Without getting closer to her, I said once more, "Sister!"

She turned away again and went to her son who was jumping up and down and swinging his arms and shouting joyfully in the rain, paying no attention to his mother and me. She took him by the arm, still jumping, and led him unprotestingly away.

I stood where I was, embarrassed, as if Janice had seen all that had taken place between Carol and myself. My clothes were drenched. The wind drove the rain into my face.

Sheepish, unacknowledged but aroused, feeling even more angry than Janice had made me feel in the cafeteria, I watched my future wife walk away from me. By the time it occurred to me to follow her, she had disappeared.

CHAPTER FOUR

For more than a year I searched the city for her, and so learned to know it as if I had been born and spent all of my life in it. I gave up my study group and discovered that it was a relief to end my ambivalent relationships with my colleagues. I attended fewer and fewer classes at the university. From Alaska, to which he had recently been transferred, Selwyn called often to repeat his exaggerated stories about women and himself. I always, now, cut these telephone conversations short. I was no longer in the mood to listen to his adventures, real or imaginary. I had my own adventures to pursue. It was as if I had come to America not to become a psychiatrist but to track down and capture Carol. And when, a little over a year after I first saw her, I saw her again in an amusement park, riding in a teacup of tulips with her son, I had to sit down to contain my excitement. I was lucky. It was a Monday, mid-morning. The park was relatively empty so I had to be careful not to let Carol see me following her.

It must have been her day off. Careful not to expose myself, I watched her for hours as she moved with her son from ride to ride, visiting the small zoo, eating hot dogs. When, finally, she and her son left the park, I followed them, discreetly, to a building not far from the one reserved by the university for its mature students in which I lived.

From the opposite pavement, I watched them enter the building, saw Carol and the doorman smiling as they spoke to each other. I saw him pat the boy's head. As soon as Carol and her son left him, I crossed the street and asked the doorman, who looked questioningly at me when I entered the building, if Mr. Selwyn was in.

"No Mr. Selwyn lives here, sir," the doorman said, and walked with me out of the building.

I began to walk to and from the university every day along the street where Carol lived. I seldom saw her. When I did, I nodded and smiled a greeting. I looked carefully for signs, of which she gave none, that she recognized me. One day in December, I turned into her street and saw her walking with her son, ahead of me. I hastened to catch up with them. I greeted them and slowed my pace. I patted the boy's head and asked him his name (it was David). I reached down, slipped my hands under his armpits, and hoisted him to my shoulders. He cried out with pleasure and surprise. I held his heels against my chest, felt his weight upon my shoulders. His arms were warm about my head. I looked at his mother and saw that she was smiling. I decided at that moment to befriend him. I would take him for walks, to movies, parks and museums. We would attend basketball and football games together. I would make him my ally in my campaign against his mother. I would pretend that I was to him the father I could not be to my sons.

I followed his mother into her apartment building and set David on his feet again before the elevator. I turned away from his beaming face, upturned to thank me, as his mother had bidden him, and said to Carol, "My name is Eugene, Eugene Coard."

She smiled, too, and said, "I'm Carol."

Immediately afterwards she pulled out a flier from her

briefcase and handed it to me. She said, "I hope you can come."

I saw that it was an announcement for an anti-apartheid rally, but the elevator had arrived before I could reply. Its doors opened noisily and David scampered into it. His mother followed him.

"Please come," she said, as the elevator began to close.

I raised my voice and promised that I would.

I did. It was held at noon in the park not far from where she and Janice had spurned me. The early December day was bright and unusually warm. The park was full of office workers sunning themselves, but the crowd standing before the microphones was small. Carol and another woman were handing out leaflets and collecting donations in cans. When she saw me she smiled and said, "I'm so glad you came."

I put a twenty dollar bill in her can.

"That will be a big help," she said. "Thanks. Everybody seems to think apartheid is over because Mandela is out of jail. They don't attend rallies anymore. They hardly make donations. Look how small the crowd is!"

I was following her through the small crowd as though she and I were a team working together and I was her protector. Her friend was already moving among the people spread out over the grass in their business clothes, as they were obviously accustomed to do when the weather permitted. When Carol headed towards them, I began to follow.

She said, "Please. Stay here. The crowd's so small."

I stood at the edge of the sparse crowd listening to the angry, metallic denunciations coming from the microphone and watched her move among the people in business suits on the grass. I told myself there was nothing more to do. I had come; Carol had seen me. The angry noises from the microphones were grating on my ears. When Carol disappeared for a moment behind a group of men standing on the lawn, I left.

I didn't see her again for three weeks. Winter, much, much colder than usual, so people said, had set in. We were both bundled up against it and, at first, I did not recognize her behind the muffler wound about her face and beneath the ski hat she wore. As we walked towards her apartment, I asked about David. She said, "He's with my mother in Alabama. I'm too busy to take care of him by myself."

I noted the "by myself". It made her seem more alone and available. I had seen no ring on her finger. Yet she lived in married student housing. I feared that she might be happily married. I preferred that she be separated, divorced or just another woman with a child to remind her of her naivete or foolish thoughtlessness.

I asked, "What about his father?"

"He's out of the country."

"Oh. Is he in the military?"

She didn't answer. I took note of that, too.

Over the next few months, I learned where her favourite spot in the library was and where I was most likely to find her in the cafeteria, sitting alone at a table, a book of political science open in front of her. She was preparing for orals. But she had reservations about her discipline. She asked me more than once, "What is the point of studying this, when one has no power to change a political system that is corrupt and oppressive?" We had many cups of coffee together, but she refused all my requests for her to come to my apartment, never once asked me to hers, and declined to attend movies, a play, a performance by the reunited Peter, Paul and Mary, or to have dinner with me.

One day, after I made my way through a sudden snow storm to the cafeteria so as to have coffee with her, and we were making small talk about the miserable weather, she blurted out, "I am, as of now, officially a divorced woman."

"What?"

"I just spoke to my attorney. I'm now no longer married."

There was no anger, resentment or relief on her face. There was only, behind its surface blankness, a very deep unhappiness. For the first time I understood how difficult the task I had set myself was. I didn't know what to say so I asked, "Was he a student, too?"

"Student and professor. But he's in South Africa now. That's where he came from."

I said, "That explains."

She nodded.

"Jason always said it was easy to demonstrate and hold rallies here. He wanted to do something more difficult. He went back to South Africa to join the guerillas." She paused, then added, "They were still fighting then. He came home from a seminar one day and said he was tired of being a mercenary, tired of preparing white Americans to continue to assume their privileged positions in this society. He was beginning to despise himself."

She took a deep breath, then exhaled. She sipped her coffee. I didn't know what to say. I waited for her to continue.

"He wanted us to go to South Africa with him. But what would I do with a three-year-old in Africa while his father was a guerilla? Jason said he had to go, whether we went or not. He was feeling too guilty. He couldn't continue to live half-safe and always dependent here while his countrymen were being killed."

She sipped her coffee, tried to compose herself. "So he went alone. Back to Africa. To fight for a future for his children. That's what he said. He left me and David here, as if there was no future in America for him to help David prepare to fight for."

She began to cry, silently. She made no attempt to wipe her tears. "How could I have begged him to stay so he could despise himself?"

She tried to smile. The tears ran down her face. "I'm not jealous anymore. I don't feel that David and I are not important because Jason left us. I don't ask myself anymore whether I was only a convenience for him while he was in America. And I don't tell myself that if I had loved him, truly loved him, I would have gone back to Africa with him. I no longer feel inadequate. He did what he felt he had to do. I only want him to be safe."

And, after another pause, "I loved him very, very much."

I said, "Dulce et decorum est…"

Carol did not let me finish. "He doesn't deserve to die," she said. "He was a good man. A good husband and father. You know? He was a refugee! He had no passport! At the time, he could not legally re-enter South Africa. I thought David and I would never lose him, that it was only a matter of time before he became American."

She shook her head slowly, wonderingly. She wiped her tears. "He could never have lived here, I see that now. He was too rigid. He didn't know how to compromise, to make concessions. He would not settle for less than what he thought he deserved. That's why I admire him. He was a good man. I only want him to be safe."

Her loyalty to the man who had walked out on her and her son was impressive. But I remembered that Ekua – standing big-bellied, silent and non-accusing – had seemed loyal, too. As time passed I had even stopped feeling grateful for her silence and inaction. I had begun to despise her for her unprotesting acceptance of what I had done to her. I considered her weak, spineless and too sentimentally manipulated by the memory of our relationship. I convinced myself, arrogantly, that I had nothing to fear from her. But Ekua had been neither weak nor cowardly. She had not been rendered incapable of action by a sentimental memory. Ekua, it seemed, had merely been biding her time. As I looked now at Carol's teary face, I asked myself how I might subvert her apparent loyalty to the man who had abandoned her and her child and turn it into a bitterness and anger from which I could benefit.

Carol said, "I didn't go with him to the airport. I couldn't bear to see him off. I thought he was going there to die and I didn't want to be his accomplice. I said goodbye in the apartment and took David with me to the park. I could hear the planes from there. Then it began to rain and I couldn't hear the planes taking off and landing anymore. I wanted it," she paused and looked at me and tried to smile, "to rain forever."

She stood up and put her book of political science in her briefcase, put on her overcoat, her scarf and her gloves. She said, "Thank you for listening."

"You're welcome," I said.

I understood that I had interrupted something important that day in the park. But Carol had made no mention of me, and I could say nothing – without giving myself away – to entice her to do so. Standing next to her, I felt as unacknowledged as I had felt when I had walked confidently up to her and she turned her back on me.

I said, "I'll walk you home."

Outside, I lowered my head against the wind-driven snow, threw an arm about Carol's shoulder and pulled her close to me. She did not resist.

"If only," I thought. "I could make her feel about me the way she feels about Jason…!"

CHAPTER FIVE

I tried to find out from Carol as much as I could about Jason. I wanted, by choosing carefully from his life as she revealed it to me, and even more carefully from my own as I had so far lived it, to construct and offer her a life she could admire by comparison. But Carol never willingly mentioned the South African again. Nor would she answer my increasingly indirect questions about him. So I was forced to create, for her admiration, a version of the life I would have liked, truthfully, to claim I had so far lived, a life that would reveal that I, too, like her ex-husband, was a good man, a good husband and father.

From this version of my life, I excluded all of the history that mattered, the personal experiences of which I was ashamed, but which no newspaper could reveal and only those closest to me could know about. I included in it all my public triumphs, the academic and professional achievements that did not really matter and which she could easily have learned from reading the newspapers of the countries where I had lived, or from speaking to people who did not know me intimately. I completed this composite of myself with other flattering and invented attributes and, daily, throughout that long, unusually cold winter, fed bits and pieces of it to Carol.

So, in time, she learned that I had given up an important position with a prestigious medical group in London in order to study psychiatry in America. But she did not know that my marriage had facilitated this appointment or that, after my divorce, I had been forced to resign from it. I told her the divorce was because of Sarah's promiscuity. Like Jason, I said, who could have continued to live in America only by despising himself, I would have despised myself if I had continued to live with Sarah. I quoted regularly from letters I was supposed to have received from England. I described the experiences, which I made up and attributed to my children, as though I had been there to witness them. I repeated again and again to Carol, as though my repetitions might make possible what I knew neither Sarah nor Ekua would ever be forgiving enough to permit, that once I had completed my studies, my son would come and live with me.

And because Jason was African, I spoke of the pleasure of eating out of the same dish with my fingers, communally with Africans in England. But I had eaten with Africans other than Ekua only once, soon after I had arrived in London. I had asked my West African host, a first-year medical student like myself, for a fork and a knife and my own plate. While he and his other African guests stood around a table and ate from a common bowl with fingers they had carefully washed, and laughed and spoke to one another in their own language, I sat on a chair, my plate on an embroidered napkin on my lap, and ate by myself. The cutlery was pure silver, the plate fine bone china; I knew this because my father, returning as a lawyer after a year in England, had brought back a set of the same kind, though after his death my mother had been forced to sell it.

After a while, a young woman left the others and came over to me. She was tall and slender. Her hair was cropped. When she smiled, her strong, even teeth flashed out of her smooth, black face. Below her loose, embroidered white bodice, she was wrapped in a multicoloured cloth that reached to her ankles. She wore sandals. In her quaint West African English accent, she told me that her name was Ekua and that she was a student nurse from Ghana who had been in England for only two weeks. I told Carol nothing about Ekua's kindness that night. I told her nothing of my other son, Ekua's and mine, who bore my name but whom I had never seen. And, of course, I never mentioned Beatrice.

After feeding Carol these carefully edited stories about my past all winter, one day in early March, when the weather had lost its grinding edge and there were intimations of spring in the air, when Carol and I were sitting in our overcoats in the cool sun outside the cafeteria, I, pretending fluster and apprehension, asked her to marry me. I had caught her by surprise. But she quickly recovered herself, smiled uncomfortably and asked, "Are you serious?"

I said I was.

"Then I must give you a serious answer. I can never marry a foreigner again."

Without thinking, I said, "I'll become an American." As soon as I said it, it seemed so obvious a weapon to use against her that I wondered why I hadn't thought of it before.

"You *are* serious!" Carol stressed the "are".

"I am."

She shook her head slowly. She smiled. "Sorry, Eugene. I can't."

After that, I brought up the idea of our marriage as often as I could. I promised to be as good a father and husband as Jason had been. I was always careful not to say better. But each time I asked her to let me take the South African's place, I hoped I underlined a little more the fact that he had abdicated it and abandoned her. Without letting her know, I applied to become an American citizen. In a separate letter, which I was not required to submit with my application, I emphasized my academic and professional accomplishments. I had to reveal that I was divorced since I did not want to risk perjuring myself. But I was not required to say why I was divorced and I was not required to mention Ekua or Beatrice. I was bound only to reveal that I had been married and was now divorced. I promised to be a good citizen, above all, to be a role model for those Americans who had too few examples of successful men and women to imitate and learn from. America and I, I wrote, could have a mutually benefiting partnership. I could be as useful to her as she could be useful to me. Within a month, I received a letter citing the exceptional services I could offer my new country and granting my request to become its citizen.

Carol was at my side when I stood in the cavernous old armoury full of other would-be citizens, and held aloft my miniature American flag and put a hand over my heart and repeated the pledge of allegiance to my new country. After the spontaneous burst of applause when the ceremony was over, after the laughter and the happy crying and the congratulations offered and joyfully received by complete strangers, because we were now Americans, I invited Carol to a bar for a glass of champagne, and she accepted, and I asked her again to marry me, and her eyes, as I had hoped they would, opened wide with astonishment.

It had been my precise intention so to surprise her. For months I had been working secretly to refine the angry and execrable accent Janice had provoked me to in the cafeteria into an instrument that might convince Carol to marry me. For months I had fallen asleep listening to talk shows, interviews, congressional hearings and debates that I had taped. For months, in the privacy of my apartment, I talked aloud to myself and listened to myself on tape after tape after tape. I had proposed to Carol, this time in an accent so flawlessly American that Janice herself, if she had heard it on the telephone, would not believe that I had not used it all my life.

Carol seemed shocked, put her hands to her face, bent forward and placed them, still cradling her face, upon the table. Then she raised her head, looked at me steadily and began softly to laugh.

"You sound," she said, "so white!"

I was too shocked to answer.

My hand was on the table. She covered it with one of hers, laughing and shaking her head and looking into my face as if I were a child who meant well but still had a lot to learn. I wanted to maintain my dignity. It had not occurred to me to imitate a mode of speech that would identify me, in America, as someone to be despised. But, watching Carol's amused face, I felt more and more foolish. I began to think that my strategy had been flawed and that I could not retain my dignity and, at the same time, make Carol want to marry me.

I pretended to be hurt. But I was also reflecting that since I had not been able to have her by guile; that since I had tried, unsuccessfully, to meet the conditions she had set for marriage to her, now she would only have herself to blame for whatever happened between us.

She said, "I will. Yes, yes, I will marry you, you poor man!" She squeezed my hand. She seemed unable to contain her amusement.

Then she said, smiling, "But, first, you'll have to learn how to speak."

CHAPTER SIX

It was not long before I was the possessor of two distinct American accents. When I spoke with the accent Carol wanted me to use, the instant recognition that I had once easily dissipated with my foreigner's accent persisted now on the faces of my listeners, and intensified, as if my accent confirmed I was the familiar object they had recognized. When I was not with Carol, I used my other American accent – the one she had laughingly described as white – because I had worked equally hard to obtain it, and spoke it so well, and did not want to give up using it. Then the look of recognition on my listeners' faces was followed by one of puzzlement. I was recognized instantly by my listeners as American, but I did not speak like an American, who looked like me, was expected to speak, and that seemed to baffle them. People wanted to know where in America I had come from. I was perverse and lied to them. I gave them the names of places I had heard or read about. I familiarized myself with details about the places in America I mendaciously told my curious listeners I had come from to make my lies believable. In this way, I began to know the country. I became more knowledgeable about it than most of its bona fide citizens.

But the private satisfaction I derived both from the initial puzzlement on the faces of my listeners, and from dispelling it with lies about my origins as an American, could not offset the unwelcome change I felt taking place within me every time I spoke as Carol wanted me to. Unable to dispel the persistent and now intensified look of recognition on the faces of total strangers, I felt I was becoming, indeed, that I had already become, someone else, someone other than myself, whom I did not know and whom my listeners expected me to acknowledge I had become. It seemed to me that I could have no name to offer as my own that my listeners did not already know, no personal past to reveal with which they were not already familiar, no private experience that was uniquely my own to interest them with: that *my* past, therefore, was no longer important and I must give it up; and my sense of myself as individual in America was unimportant, too, and I must allow myself to be deprived of it.

I tried to protect myself. I reminded myself that what my listeners saw, heard and reacted to was not real, was only a pretence, a masquerade, a device intended only to fool Carol and enable her more easily to want to marry me; and that, deep within the unseen heart of my performance, manipulating and deceiving my listeners, I was safe from them.

I could not feel safe for long. My private sense of myself could not withstand the constant public assaults upon it. Every time I opened my mouth and spoke as Carol wanted me to speak, and endured the recognizing looks of dismissal or presumptuous familiarity from complete strangers who thought me their brother, I felt more and more that I had become the American that, for Carol's sake, I wished only to seem. It occurred to me, then, that Carol had outmanoeuvred me; that, for her sake, I had foolishly given up something that was useful, even precious, to me in America – my foreignness – and exchanged it for something useless that had no power to protect me.

So, when I was with her, I spoke the way she had taught me to. But when I was not with her, I began again to speak with my foreigner's accent. I noticed all over again – but this time with anger instead of relief – how much it had the power to protect me. As if I were really an American researching what it meant to be a stranger in his own country, I watched the initial recognition of me as local product disappear from the faces of my listeners when my accent revealed to them that I was a stranger, an alien, a man from another country. However, at the very moment that I seemed to escape from the presumptions of my listeners, I felt, bitterly, more than ever appropriated by them.

The make-believe America I was pretending to be citizen of became real for me then. And its ideals which, Carol at my side, I had solemnly sworn to uphold, became real, too – and important. I was American. I had taken my new country's oath of allegiance. I had sworn to love it and honour it, to die, if necessary, for it. I should joyfully be proclaiming in my new country's accent that I was its citizen. Instead, I found myself calculatingly projecting in public the image of a man shaped by, and clinging to his past in another country.

Each time that I did so, I despised myself a little more. Each time that I lied to my fellow countrymen about my relationship to them, I felt that I abjured our common citizenship and insulted and dishonoured our country. Each time I pretended I was a foreigner, an alien, a man from another country, so as to escape from the contempt of my countrymen, from their ridicule and their fear, or from the unwarranted assumption that I was the long lost brother and ally they had been searching for, I saw myself as betraying, selfishly, merely for my personal wellbeing and comfort, our country's ideals. I felt increasing contempt for these acts of betrayal and, increasingly, contempt for the person I was who committed them.

I no more wanted to have to endure my self-contempt for masquerading as an alien in my own country than I wanted to feel that I existed only to satisfy the social and psychological needs of those who perceived me as their countryman. But self-contempt, private, and known only to myself, was infinitely more tolerable than the feeling that I could no longer affect the perceptions of me by others and that I had to submit myself to their ideas about me. What is more, playing the part of stranger in America was no longer as simple as it had once been; I felt I no longer had an appropriate stranger's accent to resort to.

Self-conscious now each time I used the English accent I had appropriated from Sarah, I saw how much I had projected with it, for my American listeners, the strange image of a man formed by, and belonging to a past, not in Africa or the Caribbean, but in Europe. I understood the curiosity I had aroused in America with it. In London, the surprise of those whom I sedulously aped had been less candid, less frank and open; there, supported always by Sarah, I had pretended not to notice it. Now, retrospectively, I acknowledged the smug, understated, slightly amused condescension that had often accompanied the compliments from people who saw themselves slavishly imitated by someone such as I, who was so obviously different from them. Now I, who had once thought of England as my home, was embarrassed by what my earnest acquisition of the language of the "best" of the English, their social manner and forms of dress, and their notions of themselves, revealed to me of my mistaken and foolish assumptions about my and my children's places in the world. I could never use Sarah's upper-class English comfortably again.

I longed for a foreign accent that would not draw attention to myself, one that, to my listeners, would seem appropriate for a man like me, and would establish clearly for them that, since I was not a local product, I could have come only from one of the other ex-slave colonies of the New World or from backward and undeveloped Africa.

But I had given up the lilting accent of the Caribbean in order to acquire Sarah's aristocratic English accent and had not bothered to learn Ekua's African-inflected English well enough to speak it convincingly. There was, now, in America, only my American accents available for me to use.

I spoke less and less in public, and to strangers only when I was compelled to. I stared back out of a blank face at them. I was often curt, not infrequently rude. Wary of being betrayed by Sarah's upper-class English, I trained myself to speak slowly. I initiated no conversation that I was not forced to initiate, asked no question I did not have to ask and answered only if I could not avoid doing so.

One day, waiting with a group of people for the light to change so I could cross the street, I heard someone close to me say, "Sir, could you please tell me what time it is?"

I paid no attention. I felt a nudge and turned to see a tall, thin, young man looking through oversized dark glasses at me. The glasses were not large enough to cover the ugly birthmark on one side of his face. His suit looked new. A red and white patterned tie stood out correctly against his solid light-blue shirt. He looked, even with the angry blemish on his face, like a confident young executive on his way to or from the office.

He said politely, "Could you tell me the time please, sir?"

I did not answer. I looked at him blankly as if I had not heard what he said. He smiled and raised his left arm in front of him and pointed to his wrist showing whitely under the cuff-linked sleeve of his expensive shirt. I smiled and exposed my wrist to show that there was no watch on it.

Then the light changed to end our little pantomime. We crossed the street and went our separate ways.

But for his hair, the colour of his skin and that livid, ugly blemish on the side of his face, he might have been me starting out, as I had confidently then thought, my new, secure life in England. And, in that split second it had taken me to smile at his assumption that I was deaf and dumb, instead of making me angry, he had made me think of a time when I had not been reduced to such bitter and resentful silence in public. It made me understand how much, irreversibly, I had already been transformed.

CHAPTER SEVEN

Carol and I were married one hot afternoon in July in the city courthouse before two of her anti-apartheid friends. Selwyn and Paul did not attend. Selwyn's company would not spare him, and Paul was in West Africa performing at the inauguration of the region's first classical concert hall which, he wrote, was even more magnificent than Vienna's Musikverein.

That night, as Carol and I consummated our wedding, she began to moan.

Melodious and drawn out, it seemed to emerge from ever more deeply within her, to rise and rise, and soar in the hot room as if it would never stop. There was a look of anguish or exaltation on her face, which moved frenziedly from side to side. Her eyes were closed. Suddenly, it seemed to me as I watched her face and listened to that sound, that it must be as unbearable for her to have to sustain it as it had become, for me, intolerable that it should end and I be deprived of the pleasure of listening to it.

But it stopped. Carol gasped several times as if there was not enough air in the hot room, then opened her eyes, a smile on her face. I buried my face in the space between her breasts, felt her hands caressing my back, thought of Jason and felt intensely jealous of the South African and tried to raise my head, as if I might see on Carol's face a memory of him. Carol, her hands behind my head, kept my face between her breasts.

"Don't move. Please!"

I didn't move.

I thought of herself and Jason together, and for the first few months of our marriage, it was for me, in Carol's hot apartment, as if she, Jason and I were always together. I felt increasingly that I shared her, that I would always share her, and, within a week I could no longer keep the South African to myself. At first, Carol laughed, said I was too jealous and did not answer my questions. But as my questions continued, she let me know – tactfully, then more and more bluntly – that it was most unpleasant for her to have to listen to them.

Naturally, I promised not to mention Jason again. Once or twice I was even able to keep my promise and any questions about Jason to myself.

But, by now, I was obsessed with the South African. My questions about him persisted. Carol began to find excuses for not making love to me. She had a headache, it was too hot, she was tired! Yet she was spending more and more time speaking on the telephone to her anti-apartheid friends.

We quarrelled!

Then, one night, when she would not let me get close to her in bed because she wanted to sleep and I was keeping her awake, I pummelled her with questions about herself and the South African.

Carol sat up, put her hands to her face and seemed to carry it painfully down to her lap. She said, "I can't take this much longer. If you don't stop, I'll have to leave. For my own sake, I have to protect myself."

I was furious that she should have chosen to speak of leaving me rather than answer my questions about Jason. I had become the American citizen she wanted me to be and could not understand how she could allow that South African, an ocean and a continent away, to come between us. But I tried to placate her. Told her I was sorry, said I was as sick as she said I was, and promised to consult one of my former study-group colleagues, who were all now practising physicians, whilst I was at least a year behind them in becoming a psychiatrist.

The next morning, she was already up and speaking on the telephone when I awoke.

"You bet," I heard her say, "they'll feel at home here. They shouldn't miss their South Africa too much."

I got out of bed and entered the living room. The day's paper was spread open on the table, and I read the headlines: "WHITE SOUTH AFRICANS ALLOWED IN BY CONGRESS". And in smaller type: "VOTE CALLED HUMANITARIAN". I heard Carol say, "This will put back the country one hundred years!"

In the early days of our marriage, when I was able to keep Jason to myself, she had seemed to like my kissing her breast through her bra. Carol, at the telephone, was in panty and bra and I went up to her and did so. She frowned and turned away from me, saying into the phone, "They'll be comfortable here, all right, and stay as long as they want… stay as long as they want. It's a shame," she added. "They'll all have passports. They're not refugees like Jason."

I said, "Carol!", left the newspaper and the chair and went up to her. She waved me off with one hand and with a finger of the other hand to her lips, and a stern face, ordered me to be quiet. So I tried fondling her breasts beneath her bra. She frowned and pushed my hand away. It was as if I was her slave and she, my mistress, and it was inconceivable that a man like me could be in love with her. I remembered Sarah.

I said, "Sarah never refused to let me fondle her."

Carol speaking to the telephone said, "I have to leave. I'll call you later."

She slammed the receiver down and turned to me. "Don't you dare compare me to that white bitch."

I said, "That white bitch never refused to make love to me."

"To you and a lot of others," Carol said icily.

It was, after all, what I had led her to believe about Sarah. But Sarah – her "white bitch" – had always made me feel I was the most important person in the world. She had fought with her parents, and some of her friends, because of me, married me against their strong objections, of her father especially. She chaperoned me carefully among her set and taught me to speak, dress and behave like them.

I said now to Carol, "Whatever else she might have done, she never withheld secrets from me."

"A good thing, too! How else would you have known she was having sexual intercourse with... was fucking others?"

I had not seen her so angry.

"I don't have to tell you anything about my life with Jason. You're not my confessor." She paused. "I loved Jason. I tried to make him happy. And he left! I understand why he did. I don't hold anything against him. But I won't ever be dependent on a man again for my happiness. I am your wife now. Not Jason's."

I said, "Then let's do what husbands and wives do."

I could hear the sounds of Carol's angry and frightened breathing. It seemed to me that I had just lost, irrecoverably, something valuable that I had possessed. It was because of this feeling of irrecoverable loss, and my fear that she now knew the power that she had over me, that I left the room, only to return to it on my way out of the apartment.

Carol was again talking on the telephone.

Neither of us acknowledged the other.

CHAPTER EIGHT

Outside, the sun was like a hammer on my head. I was in no mood to read. The library and my studio apartment were out of the question. I headed to a cinema and joined a line of people waiting to see a popular comic film. I would sit and be cool in the air-conditioned cinema for an hour or so. In the line ahead of me a young man and his female companion were reading the newspapers. I thought of the South Africans who would soon be coming in large numbers to America, of Carol's anger, and of Sarah, her white bitch, who had been my friend, teacher, lover and benefactor.

I should have learned loyalty from Sarah. By the time we were married, I had ceased to be jealous of the several partners she spoke openly to me about, with whom she had perfected the techniques she passed on to me. I was convinced that, from those lovers from her past, I had nothing to fear. Her honesty about them, the dramatic change between the promiscuous woman she told me about and the apparently protective and decidedly monogamous woman I was preparing to marry, left me in no doubt that Sarah had selected me as much, if not more, than I had selected her. When she spat in my face, I understood perfectly. That was why I had not made an excuse or sought a reconciliation.

It might have been different if I had betrayed her with another European, some barmaid in a pub, for instance, or an au-pair from across the channel. But Ekua, for Sarah, was far more dangerous. Ekua could only have represented an ancestral relationship from my past that I had deliberately excluded her from and lied about – a past to which, it would have seemed to her, I secretly clung and did not intend to abandon. I knew I could not hope to make her forgive me.

Someone touched me on the arm and said, "Excuse me, would you like some tickets?"

A blonde woman, accompanied by two little girls, was holding three tickets out to me, "My children are tired," she said. "They want to go home. We have no use for these."

I was delighted to be able to get out so quickly from the sun. I pulled out my wallet to pay her. Confidently, but gently, she put a hand on my arm.

"You don't have to pay me for them," she said. And, as I was about to accept the tickets, she added, "They were a gift. I can't accept money for them. Especially from you."

Her children were looking intently at me.

"I only need one ticket, ma'am, and I'd like to pay for it."

She said, "Don't be silly. You could always sell the other two."

I forced myself to speak slowly. But I had spoken and it was now too late to play deaf-mute.

"I'm sorry," I said.

She said, "How could you not want them? I'd never forgive myself if I gave them to someone who needed them less than you do."

People had begun to look at us. I was beginning to feel that the woman and I were on display. I was tempted to take the tickets just to end our absurd confrontation. I heard snickers. I decided not to take the tickets. I turned abruptly from the woman and began to walk away.

I felt her hand on my arm. I turned. She said, "Please take them," and there was such defeat and hurt on her now unsmiling face that I held out my hand and accepted the tickets. I heard clapping and whooping, saw her face relax, her children looking at me, and heard her say, beaming now, "Good. I'm so glad you're sensible."

I watched her walk away from me, triumphantly.

The young man with the newspaper said, "I'll buy those tickets from you if you don't want them."

I gave him the tickets. There was a small explosion of applause. I said, "You don't have to pay me."

I left. He held up the third ticket and said it was up for auction. I heard laughter and the shouts of those who were bidding for it. I turned the corner and saw a bus-stop. I was not ready to return to Carol's apartment. I joined a fat man and two teen-age boys who were waiting for the bus. They were laughing and seemed to be having a good time. The man was wearing a grey and white seersucker suit and a tie, and the boys wore T-shirts and tinted shoulder-length hair and carried skateboards. I picked up a newspaper from the empty bench and began to read it.

The man said, "Ready to camp out, mate?"

This time, I played the deaf-mute.

I heard him sing out, "You better be ready. 'Cause it's Sunday. And on Sundays buses become tortoises. Right, boys?"

He burst out laughing. The skateboarders laughed too. I felt a nudge and looked up from the paper. He had come close. His red face was moist with perspiration but otherwise he looked, dressed as he was, quite comfortable in the heat. He smiled and said, "Hot enough for you?"

I smiled blankly at him. He mouthed exaggeratedly, "Hot, hot," and removed a kerchief from his pocket, dabbed his face, fanned himself, pushed out his cheeks and blew air strongly from his mouth. I pretended I now understood him and nodded rapidly several times, then went back to my paper. I heard him tell another silly joke. He and the skateboarders laughed. He told another. And another. He seemed to be enjoying his jokes every bit as much as the skateboarders. He told a joke, nudged me and, when I looked up from my newspaper, pointed to the laughing skateboarders and exploded in a fit of laughter. I laughed.

Soon he was nudging me constantly. It was as if, deaf and mute though he perceived me to be, I had displaced the skateboarders as his primary audience; as if I were an old friend, accustomed to laughing at his jokes, whom, after a long time, he was delighted to see again.

The next time he nudged me, he pointed down the road. A man was making his way slowly towards us, stopping every now and then and swaying when he stopped. My jovial companion began to make jokes about him. Tall, thin, his hair hanging in one plait behind him, his face dirty and unshaven, the stranger stopped in front of the bus-stop and looked appraisingly at us. He stank.

I knew him well. As young boys, when no responsible adults were about, we would sneak up on drunks like him and yank them from behind and run off laughing as they fell. My jovial companion said something about the sweet smell of success, winked at and nudged me, and burst out laughing. I laughed, too, forgetting I was deaf and dumb, because I was thoroughly familiar with and disdained what I was laughing at. When my new friend made another derisive remark at the derelict's expense, and each of the skateboarders put a hand over his mouth and giggled self-consciously, as if embarrassed, I burst out laughing again.

The derelict pretended not to have heard what my friend had said about him. In a slurred voice, he asked for money to buy a cup of coffee. My fat friend threw his head back, roaring with laughter, poked me in the ribs to get my attention and asked the beggar whether he was sure that it was coffee he wanted money for. This time I waited for my cue and laughed only when the others did and signed to the beggar, like my fat friend, with arms opened wide, palms upturned, that I had no money to give him. I saw him hawk and spit, saw his spit fall on the pavement and on the tips of my shoes, and heard him utter, distinctively, the insult that could be addressed only to me. I lifted my head again and saw the enormous contempt on that broken, derelict face. I raised a hand angrily to slap it, but my upraised hand was held tightly. My jovial companion was smiling, but his eyes were stern and his grip was firm. Holding on to my hand firmly, even though my arm was down at my side again, he made a dismissive gesture with his other hand and said to the derelict, "Go on. Get away from here. You're only causing trouble."

There was a note of authority in his voice. But the derelict did not heed it. Swaying, looking at me steadily, he stood his ground and muttered, "Sure, take the nigger's side. Be a nigger-lover."

He had not finished when the fat man said, "Here," and let go of my hand. He reached into his pocket and gave some coins to the derelict.

"That's enough, you're only causing trouble. Now go. Go get your cup of coffee.'"

As the derelict took the coins and shuffled away, muttering to himself, my jovial friend laughed and put a friendly arm across my shoulder and said aloud, though obviously not to me since he believed I couldn't hear what he said, that he sure as hell didn't know what this country was coming to. I noticed that the skateboarders were whispering to each other and looking from out of the corners of their eyes at me. I felt ashamed, as if they were my sons. I said that the bus was taking too long to arrive and walked away from the bus-stop. I heard the fat man say, "Damn. We were having such a good time too, before he came and spoiled it."

A little later I heard a burst of his laughter and knew he had just told another joke. At whose expense, mine or the derelict's, I shall never be sure.

CHAPTER NINE

I was now, less than ever, ready to return to Carol. I was not ready to be reproached silently nor angrily confronted by her. I decided to head for my studio.

I was perspiring when I reached the apartment building. I saw Porter, my former study group colleague waiting in the lobby for the elevator. He was whistling a popular aria from *Aida*. He stopped when he saw me, obviously surprised. It had been a while since we had seen each other. He asked whether I had been for a walk.

I said, "Yes."

"In this heat?"

I said, "Yes."

"Must remind you of home."

I told him it did.

He said, "Like a drink? It's been a long time. We'll listen to some opera. *Aida*. You know it, don't you?" He had just come from seeing it.

I knew *Aida* well. It was Sarah's favourite opera. It was after a performance of *Aida* that I had impregnated her. I could have spent a long time discussing *Aida* with Porter. I told him I didn't know it. I declined his invitation. I said I had work to do. It was an excuse he could understand. We were no longer classmates. He and Jonathan and Reginald had outpaced me. I had fallen nearly two years behind them.

Porter said, "It's great. A good opera to start with. You'd like it." He had not the slightest idea – and I was surprised, standing next to him – how deeply at that moment I resented him.

I resented his comfort and security. I resented his lack of the anger and resentment that the woman with the tickets and the derelict's jovial protector had generated in me. I resented his ease, his confident assumption (which, when I first came to America, I had paid no attention to) that he could uninhibitedly invite me to his room to sip coffee and enjoy a recording of his favourite opera. I told myself that Porter, former colleague and future psychiatrist like myself, and I had nothing in common.

And yet, of my study-group colleagues, he was the one I had felt closest to. Jonathan's secret conversations with me about racism and anti-semitism (he always stopped and changed the subject when the others arrived), and Reginald's insistent invitations to teach with him in the ghetto seemed too much to want to implicate me in their sense of themselves as victims or victim-missionaries. Their preoccupation with fear and rehabilitation, linked to an extreme awareness of the group to which each of them belonged, seemed too restraining a grip on my reach for unrestricted personal fulfilment

I had not been taught to think of myself as victim. I had learned, late, as I climbed the path that my father had been laying down for me to follow, that my antecedents had been slaves. I understood the significance – for them – of their condition. But the fact of their slavery was, for me, irrelevant. I was not, and had never been, a slave. I was, perhaps, lucky. The society I had grown up in, made up, too, of people from Africa and Asia and Europe, had not reminded me that I was the dispossessed descendant of slaves. I had been allowed to forget.

I had grown up with the idea that I was, and was perceived by others to be, important and valuable. I had always been made to feel whole, and so I resented and felt diminished by the implicit assumptions of Reginald and Jonathan that I belonged naturally in association with them as victims. That was why I discouraged Jonathan's clandestine conversations about anti-semitism and racism, and why I always declined Reginald's invitations to teach in the ghetto.

At Thanksgiving in my first year in America, standing with Porter on the lawn of his father's estate home in the hills, watching the wide sweep of his arm as he indicated the property he was going to inherit, I had imagined, painfully, that Porter was myself and that I, with a sweep of my hand, had just indicated to him the property I stood to inherit with Sarah as my wife. Her parents took care never to be at the estate home when she and I visited. We always had it and its servants to ourselves. I had taught myself to feel very proprietary towards it.

The elevator arrived. Porter and I entered it. When we came to our floor, he said, "You're sure you won't come over for a drink?"

I said, "Yes."

"That's too bad. It would have been much more fun to listen to *Aida* with you than by myself. Some other time, perhaps?"

I nodded. He headed towards his apartment, whistling the aria. I headed for mine. Inside I closed the door behind me. In the dark and the sudden silence, I felt ashamed again that I had not broken away from the grip of my fat friend and slapped the face of the derelict whose open contempt for me, like the hidden contempt of his jovial protector, was greater than my contempt for all of them. I had wanted those wide-eyed skateboarders to see this, even though they were not my sons.

I heard a knock on the door. When I opened it, Porter seemed embarrassed. He said, "I hope you don't mind. I don't mean to pry. Is anything wrong?"

I was surprised, had no idea how much I had communicated to him of the thoughts that bothered me. I told him I was tired after my walk. And it was true that I was tired, though the heat and my walking had nothing to do with my tiredness. I thanked Porter for his concern.

"If I can help in any way…" he said, as he turned to leave. I nodded.

Late that night, when I returned to Carol's apartment, she was speaking on the telephone. She was now wearing, unusually in the hot apartment, a T-shirt and a skirt. I waited for her to end her conversation. When she put down the telephone and began to walk away as if I had not just entered the room, I said, "I'm sorry."

She stopped, turned and looked at me. There was no anger on her face. Only a neutral seriousness. She said, "I feel suddenly that I can't trust you. That I no longer know you. Is that what you want?"

"No," I said.

"I want this marriage to succeed. I haven't left. In spite of everything. But if you try what you tried this morning I won't hesitate to leave you."

I said, "I can't live in America without you, Carol." When she didn't respond, I added, "I've loved only one woman as much as I love you."

She said, "I was angry when I called her a white bitch. She may be a bitch, but she's not a white bitch. She married you, after all. But I don't want you ever to compare me to her again."

I didn't correct her. After all, Carol knew nothing about Beatrice. I promised not to mention Sarah again.

But two days later, as I stood before the mirror in the

bathroom of my studio apartment, I thought of Sarah. She was sitting naked on the edge of the bed, her legs opened wide, her head down, her fingers working. She raised her head with a look of utter absorption on her face. She laughed and said that I looked like a priest, disapproving.

Now, as I stood before the mirror, my hand pumping energetically, I felt as if I was still the young man from the Caribbean, fascinated by, but still wary of this aristocratic young Englishwoman, and I heard her say, in that voice that had seemed so cultured and full of breeding, that I was lowering my standards and was settling for a substitute that was far from adequate. And I heard Ekua laughing, asking in her delightful West African accent, why I was doing such a thing when there were so many other women in the world.

I had no answer for them. I knew only that I did not want to lose Carol, and had found an arrangement, unsatisfactory as it was, to enable me to continue my union with her. I paid no attention to the criticisms from Sarah and Ekua, those ghosts from my past, nor to the even more distant echoes of disapproval from the Caribbean.

But gradually my actions in the bathroom, from being an inadequate substitute for making love to Carol, became a substitute that was acceptable, then a habit. And one day, standing as usual before the mirror, with Carol's moan ringing in my mind, I felt I had finally achieved my liberation from her.

We continued to sleep in the same bed. We were now always civil to each other. Every day we had at least one meal together. We made love whenever she wished, during those monthly periods when she seemed willing to risk my outbursts afterwards. They did not now materialize. It was no longer important to me to make love to Carol. I was no longer jealous of the South African. I no longer thought of him as my rival. Real and tangible as Carol was, she had become as insubstantial as the man whom I had never seen, except in my jealous imagination, but who had existed so vividly for me. That was why, when I decided that she was no longer necessary to me, it was easy one night to rape her and rid myself of her and her South African ex-husband once and for all.

She was not in the apartment when I awoke the following morning. She arrived later with a removal van with two men whom I recognized as members of her anti-apartheid group. None of us spoke. As she began to collect her things, I left. A few hours later, I returned to the apartment and packed my belongings. Then, as I had always intended to do, I returned to my studio. Carol and I had been married for only twelve weeks.

CHAPTER TEN

Carol sued for divorce on the grounds of incompatibility. I chose not to contest her suit. She made clear through her lawyer how much I disgusted her. He told mine that his client wanted no alimony, no settlement of any kind. She wanted only to have nothing whatsoever to do with me.

I felt now as alone in America as, years before, I had wanted to be. Paul was always out of the country. His reputation as a violinist (he also played the flute) had soared and exploded into bits that fell brilliantly all over the world. He spent more time performing in Europe, Asia, Australia and South America than he spent living in America. The spare bedroom in my apartment was full of his postcards from the places where he performed. Each of the last two years, I had received telephone calls from him, from San Francisco and Miami, where, he said, he had gone for a day in order to meet his legal requirements as a resident alien.

Selwyn hardly telephoned. He had been transferred against his will again. He could no longer hide that he was not the important executive he wanted to be taken for. When I told him of my divorce he said, chuckling, "Use and discard. Use and discard." He complained about having to live in Louisiana, which was the latest place he had been transferred to. He said, "No international action here, man. It's like eating breadfruit and saltfish every day. The thing's good, but you bound to get tired eating it day after day after day. It's tough." I thought he sounded less and less American. I was certain he chuckled less than he used to.

Two years passed. Undistracted now, I gave myself up to what I had originally come to America to do. I became, finally, two years later than I should have been, a psychiatrist. I opened a private practice. I published some papers. I claimed they were actual case histories, but those studies of alienation were based on experiences that I concocted and attributed to patients I invented.

My invented patients trusted neither their perceptions nor the perceptions of them by others. They lived in worlds of their own and reserved for themselves the right to do in it anything they pleased. Their behaviour, from the point of view of those for whom I described it, was always outrageous and often inexplicable. One of them was a young bank clerk. Shattered when she finally met the man she had been flirting with for over a year on the telephone, she suddenly became deaf and blind. There was, I wrote, no medical explanation for her condition. The first time I saw her, she was covered with bruises. In my office, she stumbled into couches and walls. She fell over chairs. The loudest, unexpected noise could elicit no response from her. I named her illness Janice Syndrome. I claimed to have discovered it. Janice, I explained, had obviously decided she could no longer trust, nor rely upon, senses that so cruelly had betrayed her. She simply decided that she was better off without them. Her case was extreme. She was, I concluded, incurable. She had been brought too late to see me. But I suggested that if she had come to me sooner, I might have been able to do something for her.

Another of my patients claimed to be invisible. He was arrested repeatedly for nudity in public. His dream was to work, costumed as an entertaining animal, in an amusement park. He wanted, he told me, unseen within his costumes, to deride and make fun of those whom he was ostensibly amusing. But, of course, he refused to put on clothes, even in order to achieve his secret wish, and could never apply for the kind of position he wanted. In court, dressed in prison garb, he maintained that his arrests were harassment and the trial a violation of his civil rights since, but for the insulting prison uniform, no one could see him. I published a spate of such fraudulent case histories over the next few years and began to establish a quixotic, apparently attractive reputation. I was considered an exciting newcomer in American psychiatry.

One day, out of the blue, I received a telephone call from Jonathan. He invited me to lunch. I had not spoken to him in years, any more than I had spoken to Reginald or Porter. But I had followed his career, just as I had followed the careers of my other former colleagues. I had read Jonathan's papers. I knew of his excellent reputation, just as I knew of Reginald's pioneering work in the ghetto and of Porter's free clinics for the underprivileged that he held once a week in the hospital that Reginald had coaxed corporations into building. Over lunch, a week later, Jonathan told me that he felt dissatisfied working as a psychiatrist and wanted to try his hand, seriously, at becoming a novelist. He offered to sell his practice to me.

I was surprised, but only mildly. As my study-group colleague, he had always given me the impression that he trusted me more than he trusted his fellow Americans, Reginald and Porter. It was not only because of our secret conversations, which he initiated, about racism and anti-semitism, or because of his secret novel manuscripts. He treated me as an illiterate.

Though Jonathan, convinced that American art, literature and history were important sources of information for therapists of American patients, was constantly recommending books for me to read, I had single-mindedly refused to read anything that was not to do with psychiatry. He reminded me, often, of Sarah; that, as with her, I was his protégé, his special project.

Despite, perhaps because of, my fraudulent papers, my practice was growing only slowly. My patients were mostly non-European-descended Americans. However, Jonathan began enthusiastically recommending me to his mostly European-descended patients. He showed me the letter he had written about me that he wanted, with my permission, to circulate among them. He told me that they trusted his judgement and assured me that they, or most of them, would follow his recommendations. I accepted his offer.

Now, with the rich Euro-American patients Jonathan had bequeathed me, I began to immerse myself in the books that he had vainly tried to get me to read when we were students. I read American and European history. I read European and Euro-American novelists, dramatists and poets. I read Europe's and America's philosophers and theologians, their biographers and autobiographers. I visited museums to look at European and Euro-American art. I wanted to understand my new patients not simply as people formed and shaped in America, but as Americans influenced by the traditions of the Europe they or their ancestors had fled from.

But the research that I undertook to better understand the patients I had inherited from Jonathan led me, inevitably, to examine my own condition as an American. In the monographs and books that I published during this period, I wrote of my patients as people who had a memory of deprivation and persecution and were determined, in their new environment, not to be deprived or feel persecuted again. I explained the psychical need of my fellow Americans from Europe to assert themselves and be dominant in their new country. But, behind the neutral, academic tone of those publications, was my firming acknowledgement (and consequent despair) that as my fellow countrymen had fled Europe and come to America to be powerful and white, so I had come to be powerless and black; and that the only way to escape from my condition was to follow the European example and flee America as they had once fled Europe, long before my own semi-enforced departure.

But I no longer wanted to flee America. I was establishing a reputation as an important and influential American. I was important – despised representative though I was to some Americans – precisely because I was so deeply involved with things American. I could not imagine myself as important, influential or relevant in any other country. Besides, even though I told myself that I had overcome my obsession with Carol, I felt that to leave America would be to abandon her. I was definitely not now about to leave America.

I began, instead, to research the ways in which the powerful and the powerless, the strong and the weak, the dominant and the dominated have, historically, lived well together. I explored the psychology of the slave-driver who was himself a slave, of the colonial administrator, himself one of the colonized, of the leader from among the conquered who accepted appointment by those who occupied his country. I became an expert in the psychology of the collaborationist in all his guises and disguises.

I did not call him a collaborationist. I used words such as shrewd, practical and pragmatic to describe him. I underlined his firm grasp of reality, his unsentimental ability to read and make the best use of the historical moment. Consensus, compromise, the absence of distracting, unattainable ideals, or self-deluding fantasies, were, I wrote, what made such figures seize and successfully manipulate the important roles that the impersonal forces of history created for them. It was as a result of writing that book and of the revulsion for myself that I felt after I had finished it, that my attitude to my Euro-American patients changed.

I had observed, in the American novels I had read, that when Americans from Africa and from Europe both appeared, they became blacks and whites, but that in books where Americans from Africa did not appear, Americans from Europe ceased to be simply white and, no matter how long they or their ancestors had lived in America, became Anglo-, Dutch-, German-, Italian-, Jewish-, Catholic- or every other kind of hybrid American that reflected where in Europe they or their ancestors had come from.

I decided that I would deprive my patients who were Americans from Europe of this comforting hybrid sense of themselves; to persuade them that their attachment to cultural, ethnic and religious origins in Europe was sentimental and self-deluding and served only to mask their deep fear of confronting themselves as American; and to force them to accept that their essential condition as Americans was necessarily to be white, in opposition to those of us who were not. No matter what they came to see me about, I made it my business to underline for them, insistently (though in all kinds of unobtrusive ways), the ever-present danger to themselves of Americans like me who, educated or uneducated, rich or poor, criminal or law-abiding, forced them, by our mere presence, to give up their cherished, hybrid notions of themselves and become, necessarily and often brutally, for their own protection, American and white. I did not blame them for this deplorable but unavoidable change. Instead, I emphasized the difference between the cultured European-Americans they liked to think they were and the brutally pragmatic American whites we had forced them to become. I wanted, no matter how diverse their cultural, religious, political and ethnic origins in Europe might have been, to entrap them as inescapably within their single condition of American whiteness as I felt entrapped in my single condition of American blackness. I wanted to make them as destructively and self-destructively white as possible, to make racists of those who were not, and make more racist those who already were. I was careful always to use words like barbaric, uncivilized and savage to describe those of us who forced this unwanted transformation upon them. But, by stressing the ugliness of the transformation itself, I ensured that they asked themselves whether they had not become, through no fault of their own, and merely to protect themselves from us, brutal and barbaric and savage, too. The idea was to mangle them psychologically, confuse them about who they were, raise questions in their minds about who they otherwise might have been. I wanted to make American whiteness necessary, but ugly and something they should be ashamed of, and at the same time render them dependent upon those of us who forced this self-preserving whiteness upon them. I wanted to debase them and to make them come willingly to be debased by me. I convinced them that I was the man to help them cope with the unavoidable curse of being white in late-twentieth century America. I made them dependent on me. In this way, I satisfied my deepest need not to feel dominated by any of them.

My practice grew. I was often overworked; I sometimes saw the same patient three times a week. I was becoming a very rich man. I was becoming rich in America by alleviating anxieties that I had myself reinforced or provoked in those referred to by others, privately, as bohunks, dagos, kikes (I list them alphabetically because I want to insult none of them in particular), micks, polacks, tockos, wasps; as well as a host of others whom it would be tedious to mention.

CHAPTER ELEVEN

It was during this period of public success and private and vengeful satisfaction (which even so did not alleviate my discomfort as an American) that, one night, I switched on the television and saw Carol again. Her chest was heaving. Her eyes blazed. As the camera moved slowly closer to her, she whispered fiercely, her face more angry than I had ever seen it, that no white brat, none whatsoever, would cripple her son and get away with it.

The newsman explained. Carol had slammed a door so violently on a child's fingers that two of them had to be amputated. In his neutral newscaster's voice he went on to say that, a week earlier, a playmate had accidentally slammed a door on her seven-year-old son's fingers, but that the playmate was not the youngster Carol had maimed. I sat up in my chair. My heart beat violently. I heard the newscaster say, in his bored voice, that he would keep us abreast of that late-breaking story. It was now eight years since I had left Carol's apartment for the last time. Unless she had known another man while we were married or during the months immediately preceding or following our marriage, she and I had a son and she had told me nothing about it.

I thought I had forgotten her. But, that night, I jumped awake from a dream that would recur until the end of her trial, in which I always saw her, eyes closed, mouth open with awe and wonder, as if impaled against the bare wall of a large, empty room, by a man whose back was always towards me. When I fell asleep again, I found myself in a large empty room – all white: white walls; white carpet, immaculately clean; and with white lighting so skilfully arranged that no shadow showed. There was a white crib in the centre of the room. Under the gossamer lace that covered it, I saw my American son, the one I hadn't known I had. He seemed to be sleeping. I approached the crib, lifted the veil and saw that his hands, lying on the white sheet on either side of his face, had been cut off neatly at the wrists.

This time, I did not go back to sleep. I thought of his half-brothers, the half-European and the half-African, living with their mothers, fatherless, somewhere else in the world. I thought of them as safe. I felt good, worthwhile. As if their safety was the result of my own deliberate planning. I thought of parents and their children during that long sleepless night, and, in particular, of the parent I had read about, a father who loved his daughter enough to set her ablaze because he did not want to hand her over, as the court had ruled, to his ex-wife whom he despised. Alone in the dark, I acknowledged the enormity of Carol's contempt for me, and decided to respect it.

I followed her story in the newspapers and on the first day of her trial, headed for the courthouse. I should have gone earlier. The line of people waiting to enter the courthouse stretched for blocks. Policemen, on foot and on horseback, watched them. I took my place in the line and asked the nearest policeman what my chances were of getting into the courthouse. He asked what trial I wanted to attend. I told him. He thought my chances were pretty good. It would have been different, he said, if I had wanted to attend one of the other trials. I asked him what they were about. He said that one was about a man who had killed thirty teenagers over several years and buried their bodies in his basement. He had eaten the hearts of some and regularly drank beer out of the skull of one of them, which he kept in his refrigerator. "Pretty gruesome," the policeman said. I asked about the other trial. He said it was about two hunters who had killed a man in the woods.

While he was telling me this, another policeman announced through a bullhorn that there were no spaces left in the rooms where those other two trials were being held. Many of the people who were waiting to enter reluctantly left and, as a result, it was not long before I was next in line to enter the courthouse. An old man in front of me, who was leaning on a cane, and whose veins showed bluely through the skin of his hands, was permitted to enter. But, as I prepared to follow him, the policeman barred my way, saying the room was now full and I would have to wait for someone to leave before I could be allowed in.

I stood indecisively for a moment. I did not want to miss the trial. I had taken my first vacation in years in order to attend it. Suddenly, the old man emerged from the courthouse and hastened past me, muttering angrily to himself. I was allowed to enter.

Once inside the courtroom I understood. The people attending Carol's trial had arranged themselves in two groups. On one side sat her supporters who, in all their complexional variety, were black. On the other side were her adversaries. They were nearly all white. At the far end of the back row of seats, on the side of the room where Carol's supporters sat, was the seat that the angry white man had made available to me. I gratefully took his place.

The man sitting next to me introduced himself. He was immediately friendly, as if he and I had known each other for a long time. During breaks in the trial he made supportive remarks about Carol that I felt he expected me to agree with. He wore glasses. There was a gap between his upper canines. His hair and short beard were white and curly. He made me feel, uncomfortably, that I was part of a team supporting Carol and concerned only with exonerating her.

The trial began. The prosecutor said he would show that Carol was an unfit mother, an angry, vengeful woman who had been divorced at least twice, who by her horrible deed had pushed back the cause of race relations in America by at least a hundred years. Because of her, two American children, one white the other black, would be maimed and malformed for the rest of their lives. He said many other negative things about Carol and ended by saying that she was dangerous and should be jailed for a very long time.

Carol's lawyer compared her to a computer. The computer was lucky, he said. When it broke down, it simply ceased to function. All the information stored within its memory became, at once, useless and unusable. It had simply to be fixed. But when we break down, all the information we have received from our society about ourselves; about ourselves in relation to it; about ourselves in relation to others; all of that stirs, rises unbidden to the surface of our legally imposed civility and is at hand for us to use. When his client committed the horrible act for which she was now before the court, she had been temporarily insane. And it was precisely because she had broken down that she could perform most efficiently. Like those two white hunters being tried at this very moment in another courtroom…

The prosecutor jumped to his feet and objected. The judge sustained his objection. She asked Carol's lawyer to stick to the matter at hand. And, in a calm voice, he did. Everything, he said, that his client had been programmed for, even before she was born, all the information that her society had transmitted over centuries to her, as its slave, its

74

non-person, its fraction of a person, its inferior, despised and disparaged citizen, all that information about who she had been, was and could be, far from being useless and unusable at the moment of her mental breakdown, her temporary insanity, had simply been uncovered from where it lay, deep within the recesses of her mind, and put brilliantly, instinctively, to use. His client, he would show, was logical when she performed the horrible act for which she was being tried. She was logical, insane, like the society she belonged to. She was not guilty.

On the second day of the trial, I arrived early at the courthouse and sat in an unoccupied seat among Carol's adversaries. I was unwilling to join the game that the people in the courtroom had set up for themselves. No one sat in the row I was sitting in until all the other rows were occupied. And no one, throughout that day, sat on the seats next to or immediately in front of and behind me.

For the rest of the trial, I decided by a flip of a coin where in the courtroom I would sit. The coin decided. I sat wherever it commanded me. I endured the angry stares of Carol's adversaries when I sat among them. I accepted that her supporters, including the man with the short, curly white hair and beard, who had a gap in his upper canines, should now be less than friendly to me when the coin made me sit with them.

The trial lasted for two weeks. Carol's lawyer's strategy was to make his client a victim and a martyr.

"The prosecutor," he said one day, midway through the trial, "has spoken of revenge. But revenge is deliberate. Revenge is premeditated. Revenge is planned and calculated. My client's act was instinctive. Spontaneous. She did not know her victim. She had not sought out and stalked the child who had accidentally maimed her son while they played together in order to maim him. She had not waited for the right moment to smash his fingers. I, too," he said, "had I been helpless and vulnerable enough, could have been her victim.

"Her act, bursting out from beneath our precarious civility, and exploding spectacularly for us to see, was a horrible act. We are repulsed by its ugliness. We swear it is unusual. We protest that it is an oddity. Thank God, we say, that the rest of us are not like that.

"But we are. Ask those hunters, convicted now, whom the prosecutor doesn't want me to talk about. Given the right circumstances, we all are. As Americans. We cannot help but be. If we have to be thankful, it should not be to God, but to this woman sitting before the court for the lesson she has given us about our innate capacity to be, no matter how frighteningly, or how shockingly, our cultural selves.

"My client should never have married that South African," the lawyer told the jury. I looked at Carol when he said this. I wanted to see how this strategy to save her would fit with her deep love for Jason. Her lawyer blamed her for marrying him. At the same time, he sought to show that her decision to marry Jason was not her choice alone, that, like a computer, she had already been preprogrammed to make it.

She had been a brilliant student of Romance Languages, a student, that is, of national and cultural psychology. She should have known the danger of marrying a man forced to flee his country in despair, who yet loved it so much that he refused to become citizen of the one that had welcomed him. She should have known the potential of such a man to make unhappy those who were close to him.

Yet she had married him. Surrounded at her prestigious university by so many talented Americans, she had reached out to that dissatisfied and necessarily unhappy exile, not as an exotic lover in an affair that would end sooner or later, but as a mate to spend the rest of her life with, to be the father of her children and her partner in the serious business of rearing responsible future American citizens.

She might have imagined she was in love. But, like Americans before her who had discarded their American names for African ones, who had changed their religions, styles of hair and modes of dress, who had clutched at symbols from another continent in order to draw attention to their alienation and marginality in their own, she had merely been sentimental. She imagined she had something in common with that African exile. She had behaved as if she saw in him a reflection of herself to which, like a caged bird, she was foolishly attracted. Foolishly, because, after he left her, she would never be the same again.

"I do not," he said on the last day but one of the trial, "under the circumstances, blame this man for leaving his wife. I cannot fault him for being a patriot. I cannot hold it against him that he loved his wife, but loved duty and his country more."

But after the South African left, the intelligent woman, the first of her family to attend university, who had been preparing herself to serve in her nation's service, lost direction, became confused, found herself adrift without national purpose on a disturbed sea of private emotion.

She helped to organize anti-apartheid rallies. She helped stage events to raise money for anti-apartheid agencies. She fought with her fellow Americans intellectually, sometimes physically, at demonstrations and counter-demonstrations. Energies that she once devoted to her family and to preparing herself to serve her country, she now devoted to promoting actively another country's affairs. Here, in this country, she behaved as if she belonged to another; as if American and living in America, she had become African.

She was not the first, nor would she be the last, to turn away from a brutal American reality and look towards another continent for solace. She was not the first, nor would she be the last who, when that distracting look abroad did nothing to solve problems at home, would react destructively to the reality she had sought to avert her eyes from. Even years later, whenever she applied for a job, her interviewers always questioned her closely. They thought her dangerous and subversive. She had to settle for positions for which she was more than qualified. The future, the life for which she had been preparing, became less and less open to her. She married again. Another foreigner. She divorced again. She dropped out of school. She had now two children to take care of.

One day, she returns home from an unsuccessful job interview and sees an ambulance in front of her apartment building. A playmate has slammed a door shut on her son's fingers. They don't, it turns out, have to be amputated. But his hand will never be normal again and for her, who had left him alone, it must have been a perpetual reproach. A week later, the first ones to arrive on the scene find the door still closed on her innocent victim's fingers. The air is rent by his terrible screams. Carol is sitting on the steps before the brownstone house, her face in her hands.

Carol's lawyer paused. He was perspiring. His face was red from his efforts to prove Carol a victim. He was a young fellow alumnus who had volunteered to defend her free of charge. From the second day of the trial, he had been protected by the police because people had threatened to kill him.

"My client was mad," he continued, "when she performed that horrible act. Like an athlete, like a soldier, like those white hunters, crazed with drink, who shot their black countryman in the woods, my client has merely reproduced, instinctively, a behaviour she learned and internalized over years of training. If we are shocked by what she has done, we should also admire it – as we would admire the daring, unexpected dropshot on the tennis court that startles us into applause; the leap on the concert stage that makes us gasp and hold our breath; the uppercut we hardly saw that fells a boxer like a log. None of us should assume the right to punish her!"

That night, it took me a long time to fall asleep. Early the next morning, I found myself standing before the courthouse, spinning my coin and dutifully taking my place, as it commanded me, among Carol's adversaries.

"I cannot," I heard Carol's lawyer begin, "fault the patriotism, the courage and the honour of this man who abandoned his wife and child and gave up a career in America in order to fight to regain his country. I can only admire him. But," he continued, "the consequences of his patriotism and of his extraordinary private sacrifice has been disastrous for my client. For it made possible her marriage to a beast." And pointing to where I sat, surrounded by empty seats, he called me a parasite, a vulture, a predator of the worst kind. I had never loved Carol. I had wanted only to sleep with her.

His face was redder than I had ever seen it; his finger was accusatory. It was as if I, not Carol, had perpetrated the crime she was charged with. I began to squirm in my seat. What else had Carol told him about me? But, apparently, the well-trained advocate and diligent researcher had not relied only upon Carol's information. Raising his voice even higher, he revealed to the court aspects of my life in England that only Sarah and Ekua, or their lovers, confidants and lawyers, could have known.

I was mortified.

The South African refugee, he repeated, was an honourable man. But I, he said, had abandoned my country. I had not been driven out either by war or by economic, social or political necessity. I was not persecuted, and my country, because it was undeveloped, could only have benefited from the services of a man trained as I was. I had given up a dignified life as a respected and responsible citizen in my native country and had accepted to become, because of a woman, a despised citizen of America.

The entire court seemed to gasp. I do not know whether it was because of the reference to Carol, or because of the notion, expressed in a court of law, that a citizen of America could be despised. From both sides of the aisle I heard shouts of "Shame!", "Traitor!", "Spy!" Someone screamed, "Go home!" Another, "America, love it or leave it!" The judge was gavelling furiously and policemen were scurrying about trying to restore order.

I sprang to my feet. I wanted to say that I *had* lusted after Carol and *had* betrayed Sarah and Ekua, but that I had not slammed the door on that innocent child's fingers. Instead, I heard myself screaming as loudly as I could that I loved my country and that it was an honour and a privilege for me to belong to it. That all I wanted was to feel as loved by it as I loved it. To be, unambiguously, its loyal citizen.

"Your Honour, I admire the African's patriotism. But I don't want to feel, like him, that I must fight and possibly kill or be killed by my fellow countrymen, for the right to be our country's full citizen."

I felt myself grabbed from behind. I turned, prepared to fight. I saw the policemen's uniforms and did not resist. One of them roughly pulled my hands behind my back and cuffed them.

The courtroom became orderly again. The judge ordered that I be brought to her. There was now a policeman on either side, one in front of, and another behind me. From her high seat, the judge asked why I had disrupted her court. I told her I had lost my head. I had been frightened by the shouts of "Spy", "Traitor," and "America, love it or leave it". I had felt I threatened by every one sitting in the courtroom.

I said, "Those people…" and tried to point out both Carol's supporters and adversaries and discovered that I couldn't, and remembered that my hands were manacled behind my back. It seemed to me that I had finished the sentence, but that only the judge and the policemen guarding me heard what I had said. It was only when the judge spoke and I could barely hear her that I realized that the microphones were off and that whatever I said now was only among the judge, the policemen and myself.

I began to shout. I repeated what I had begun to say when the microphones went dead, "Those people up there who form their excluding groups…" I felt a hand clamped firmly over my mouth.

The judge said, "There's no need to shout."

And, indeed, there wasn't. Her voice was loud and authoritative again. The microphones were on once more. The judge asked the policeman to remove his hand from over my mouth and asked me why I should not be charged with contempt of her court.

I said that my American son was maimed for life and I had been unable to prevent it. I had wanted a son who was whole but would have to be satisfied with one who was not. I broke down and began to cry. I saw the judge looking sympathetically at me. I seized the opportunity.

"Your Honour, what can my son do with his hands amputated at the wrists? He can never play the violin or the piano. He can never be a surgeon. He can never touch the face of the woman he loves."

"Objection!" Carol's lawyer shouted.

"Sustained," the judge said.

Then, without answering my question, she gavelled and called for order, and promised to hold in contempt anyone who disrupted her court again. She asked the policeman to escort me back to my seat and told Carol's lawyer he could continue. And calmly this time, and without pointing to where I was, back among the empty chairs, he said he had only this to say about me – that I had no morality, no ethics, no loyalty to anyone, group or country and that he was only sorry that his client had not known that she, like America itself, would have been better off without me.

I awoke from my dream then and realized that I had either not heard the alarm or had slept through it. I dressed and rushed to the courthouse. But the door was closed and the line of people waiting to enter stretched for more than a block. I never made it inside the courtroom on that last day. Carol escaped. Her lawyer had succeeded in making her a victim. I read the details in the papers the next day. She was found not guilty by reason of insanity and confined to a mental institution.

I was not displeased with the verdict. For the first time since she had left me, I felt fully at ease, although she was not with me. Locked up in that institution, from which only those trained such as I was could free her, she was unavailable to me and to others. The walls of her asylum were as effective as a chastity belt. I could sleep now without jumping awake from punishing dreams in which I watched her stand against a wall, mouth agape with awe and wonder, while unknown men, their backs always to me, made marvellous love to her.

PART TWO

CHAPTER TWELVE

The morning after Selwyn's call about Red, I awoke tired and depressed. I had spent most of the night retracing my past as though news of Red's death had opened a path for me reluctantly to follow. I finally fell asleep. At about four o'clock! It was eight forty-five now. Peggy hadn't called, and I had missed my first patient. I phoned my office and asked Jennifer, my secretary, to cancel my next two appointments. Then I called the doorman on the intercom and asked to speak to my driver, Franz. I apologized to Franz for making him wait and asked him to come back for me in an hour.

Franz was an important part of my pact with America. He was an immigrant like myself and had come, in his forties, from somewhere in Eastern Europe – where exactly I didn't know, since I made it a point not to be personal with him. He was now nearly seventy. His chest was still like a box; his hair, thick and white. His Caucasian nose – sharp, pointed – was the sort of nose once used to illustrate anthropology textbooks.

For years he had been my pilot in the city. I called upon him to drive me through it, and to and from its airports at all hours of day and night. He never complained. He and I had a very special relationship: because of him, I did not, for example, have to put up with taxi drivers refusing me as a fare, and he paid no interest on the loan I gave him to buy his taxi cab company. When, after an hour I came to the lobby, he was talking to the doorman. I apologized again as he took my briefcase and we walked together to his taxi.

He said, "The strike is over, Doc. They announced it on the radio this morning. It will take a long time to clean up the mess."

I had not heard this news; in the streets of the neighbourhood where I now lived, garbage was not permitted to accumulate. Those of us who lived there relied on our own private garbage collection service. But speaking of garbage reminded me again of Red's "neighbourhood" and his funeral there tomorrow.

We got into the car and after we had gone a few yards I said, "Oh, by the way, Franz, I have a funeral to attend."

"OK, Doc. Just tell me where and when."

"Tomorrow at ten," I said. "We'll drive to the funeral home. You'll wait for me. Then we'll drive to the cemetery."

I watched his face in the rear-view mirror. I hesitated, but when he caught my eye in the mirror, I told him where the funeral home was. He looked away from me, and down at the road. He was silent for a moment. Then he said, "I'll take you there, Doc, but I won't wait for you. You know how it is. You listen to the news, too. Anyone else, I don't even go in."

He had not refused to take me anywhere before. It seemed it wasn't so easy for him to refuse me now. His face was solemn, his eyes avoiding mine.

"Sorry, Doc. It's not my fault. We both know how things are."

"I don't want to go there anymore than you do, Franz," I said. "But it's for a friend. A very old friend. It's the least I can do."

His eyes remained focused on the road ahead of him.

He said, "I wouldn't go in there. Not even for an old friend, Doc. But then an old friend of mine wouldn't live there. With you, it's different."

He paused. I was accustomed to his pauses during our conversations. But this pause was different. I sensed that it did not simply mark a lull in our conversation. Franz continued, "I know a man. Good driver. Very reliable. Friend of mine, too. He would wait for you as long as you want."

"You've never refused me before, Franz," I said.

He said, "I'm old, Doc. It's time for me to retire."

He had said this before. Always, he had looked in the rear-view mirror and smiled, saying it. And, always, I had answered him, "You'll be driving for the next hundred years, Franz. You know that."

I said so now. In the past, his eyes would have sought mine. He would have smiled in the mirror back at me. I felt suddenly cut adrift and exposed to all in the city that he had, until this moment, insulated me from.

He said gravely, "It's time, Doc. You want a replacement for me. That man, he's a good man. You'll like him."

He had made up his mind. There was nothing I could do. He didn't need the handsome salary I paid him. His taxicab company was very successful. He could repay, easily, not only the loan, but – if there had been, though there wasn't – any interest on it. Franz and I had been more than borrower and lender. We had been partners and I had to admit that he was much more important now to me than I was to him.

"Franz?"

"Doc."

"Is he as good as you?"

He heard the appeasement in my voice. He looked in the mirror at me and smiled.

"He's excellent."

CHAPTER THIRTEEN

By 4:30 I had seen all but one of my scheduled patients. The one was a forty-five-year-old divorced woman whose name I feel it prudent not to mention and whose ancestors included North African Jews, English Catholics and Irish and Italian Protestants. We had reached the stage in her treatment where I had made her sick with apprehension about what would happen to her if people like me disappeared from America. I had convinced her that in such a society she would no longer be identified as white, in contrast to those of us who obviously were not. For Americans like herself who could only group themselves in terms of ethnic, religious or national classifications derived from Europe, there would be no group for her, ancestrally mixed as she was, to belong to. I had rendered her so pathologically fearful of being excluded, marginalized and discarded that the first thing she always did when she entered my office was to hug me and say, "I love you, Doc. I hope you never die. Thank God for people like you."

She was so obsessively punctual for her appointments that, when she did not show up on time, I knew better than to expect her. But I was concerned. I did not want to risk having her suffer a relapse. I asked Jennifer to call and remind her that she had missed a session and should reschedule another for as soon as possible. Jennifer then gave me the list of the next day's patients and I saw, with some pleasure, that Walker's was the first name on the list. I hoped he would show up for this appointment. He had missed the last three or four.

He was the only patient left from those early days of my practice when I was obsessively inventing fictional patients. One day, I opened the door to my office, and there he was, standing before it. His camel hair coat was like the one hanging in my office closet and I recognized his cheery silk necktie as similar to the one I had chosen not to wear that morning. He was about my height and, though he was bigger about the chest and shoulders, I had, for an instant, the slightly unnerving impression that I was looking at a reflection of myself.

"Mr. Bellow?" I had called out and smiled at the man standing in front of me – whom I knew not to be Bellow.

The man said, "Walker. I.M. Walker." He took my free hand and began to shake it.

I said, "Hi, Mr. Walker. My next patient is Mr. Bellow…"

Walker said, "I gotta see you, Doc. Now. It's urgent."

"I'm sorry, Mr. Walker," I said, and looked past him and called out again into the waiting room,

"Mr. Bellow? Mr. Bellow?" I saw Mr. Bellow sitting apart from my other patients, nattily dressed, with his elfin face and his sad eyes with the flesh-pouches under them. He was one of my few patients at this time who was white. He waved a hand nonchalantly and said, "That's all right, Doc. I can afford to wait. Let the gentleman tell you his story."

So Walker and I entered my office together.

At that first session, he told me a jumbled tale of armed, masked men in white robes springing upon him out of the dark; of crosses flaming on the front lawn of his home; of bullets fired into its walls and bombs thrown through its windows. He wanted me, he said, to help him cope with the anxieties those events caused him.

I was so taken aback by this obvious appropriation of public information for his private purposes that I laughed outright at him. I told him I could not help him if he merely repeated, as if they were his own, experiences from the national past, that he had heard or read about. I could work with him only as a man with a private history who brought me experiences that had actually happened to him; as an individual, not a national product; as a person, not a member of a group.

Walker paid no attention to me. In subsequent sessions, he continued to behave as if he had no coherent memory of a private life that I could try to help him understand.

He was, for instance, at different times, sometimes a Christian, sometimes a Jew, also, sometimes, a Muslim. In his white robes, he praised Allah and spoke bitterly of having been excluded from churches and synagogues when he was a boy, even though he was a baptized Christian, and his mother had been a maid for Jews who had advised her to circumcise him. But for all his complaints he was patriotic. Once, when I said something – I no longer remember what – that seemed to him to raise questions about his status as an American, he answered testily, "I'm American same as you, Doc. This is my country. I belong here."

I was, at the time, anarchically chronicling my unhappy experiences as an American and marketing them packaged cosmetically as the experiences of others. I could not understand Walker's morbid, self-serving patriotism, his schizophrenic relationship with himself and with our country, his apparently wilful suppression of any private life important enough for him to remember and talk to me about. He behaved as if the only way he could obtain significance for himself was by identifying himself as national victim of the most shameful events of our country's history. I understood his mythomaniacal need to draw attention to himself and grasp at a status and importance that was otherwise generally denied him, but, as a therapist, I could not help him. However, at this point in my career I had not yet begun to benefit from my fictitious case histories, so I cultivated him as my patient and was grateful for his fees. In the process, I became very fond of him.

I was remembering this when Jennifer buzzed to say that Mrs. Lynch had insisted on coming to see me. Without delay the door opened and Fiona Lynch entered my office.

"I did it," she said.

I was cautious. I didn't dare believe what I wanted to. I invited Fiona to sit down.

"Did what, Fiona?"

"I killed him."

My heart began to beat quickly. "Mr Johnson?" I asked quietly.

"Yes. I shot him."

My heart lit up triumphantly. But I did not get up and throw my arms about her shoulders.

"His wife, too."

"The woman in the wheelchair?" I asked. "The invalid? The one you said you felt sorry for?"

Fiona nodded. She said, "May I use your telephone?"

Not moving in my chair, I watched her as she began to flip through the pages of the telephone directory.

The plush-carpeted corridor of her new apartment building, she told me, had quickly become a jungle for her. She often did not hear Mr Johnson until he was upon her. Then, softly, always softly, even though there was never anyone else to hear him, he aimed his special greeting at her.

When Fiona first came to me, I had immediately detected the Scottish brogue beneath her new American accent. When she told me of her trouble with her new neighbour, Mr Johnson, I immediately became interested. I was writing a book – as a warning to white Americans – about the dangers to them of playing out, in America, the divisive national, ethnic or religious antagonisms that had been so destructive in the old continent. A chapter about Scottish Fiona duking it out with the Anglo Johnson would have fitted nicely into the book.

But when she told me the names Mr. Johnson called her – "nigger-lover", "prostitute" – I was angry that she had chosen to come to me. I had long rejected the role of victim. I had my own victims now. I didn't want to be bothered by things I had long since painfully worked my way through. I wanted to send Fiona to Reginald in the ghetto, or to the free clinic that Porter held there for those whom he called underprivileged. But Fiona would probably not have been welcomed in the ghetto; she was underprivileged only through her marriage to a fellow student from the West Indies whom she had met in Scotland. I asked her if she knew what my fees were. She didn't. I told her. I had doubled them, but she didn't flinch, and I was stuck with her.

At first I had not known how to deal with Fiona. I could not make whiteness indispensable to one for whom it was obviously already dispensable. I could not heighten her fear – since she obviously did not possess it – that she might not always be white. I was baffled about what to do with her. Then she told me about her dreams. Horrible dreams, she called them. Dreams in which she stalked Mr Johnson night after night after night. She cornered him, just as he cornered her in the corridor, and shot him in the face. But nothing happened. And as she shot and shot, her rage and her frustration growing, his smiling, confident, handsome face only got bigger and bigger, until it engulfed her within its cottony softness, its terrifying warmth. She always woke up then, she said, and was unable, for a long time, to fall asleep again.

Now I had something to work with. I reinforced Fiona's sense of herself as an individual free to do whatever she thought was right, regardless of the perception of her actions by others. I set out, that is, to reinforce her idea – which by her marriage she had demonstrated – that she was an individual, and not just another member of a group. I was delighted to make her feel that in America she was, like me, a tribeless outcast and that she was morally and ethically free to devise her own solutions to the problems America placed before her. She had told me about her domestic unhappiness. Of Tom, her physicist husband, devoted to his classified research and proud of his contribution to the cause of a free world, so much so that when she, frightened by Mr Johnson and tired of her dreams, asked him to leave America, he refused, saying his work was too important. This left her virtually alone to rear Mike. She was bitter that her happy marriage in Scotland seemed to have been just a preparation for being a wife to a black man and mother to their black child in "this wretched country".

The words were hers. She had spoken to me of her alienation from the other mothers with whom she spent afternoons in the park, watching her child play with theirs, unremarkable as yet to those he played with, but remarkable to her, and to the other mothers who pretended he was not. All the time, she would be chatting amiably with them, but thinking bleakly about his future. She had never said to those friendly women that she was angry and resentful because she despaired of her son's future in this country. She felt herself a hypocrite and, in some sense, their accomplice, because she was sitting and talking pleasantly with them, as if there was nothing for her to be fearful and resentful about, and the future they contemplated together was equal for all of their children.

She had told me how ashamed she felt because she

sometimes wanted to lay down the burden of being wife to Tom and mother to Mike. She was tired of being constantly stared at whenever she walked with them in public; wanted, sometimes, to go away and be by herself, alone, forever.

She had told me of her feelings of being imprisoned in America and chained to Tom; how she doubted her ability to raise her son adequately on her own; of her feelings of dependency, inadequacy; how miserable, lonely, afraid and unhappy she was, tired of constantly feeling that her child was imperilled, and herself and her family constantly de-meaned. She wanted to leave America and be rid of this need to protect her son and preserve herself, to have nothing more to do with this obsession with blackness and white-ness. She had told me all of this and I had sought to reinforce in Fiona the idea that she should kill Mr Johnson because it was exactly what I myself would have wanted to do.

I made progress slowly. Fiona was deeply Lutheran. There were severe limits to what she believed she was permitted by God do. That was why her dreams of killing Mr Johnson were horrible to her. She resisted my attempts to make her a murderess, and I had for some time concluded I could not persuade her to kill Mr Johnson. I was glad now that he was dead, but I could take no credit for his death. I wondered what had persuaded Fiona to kill him.

She said, still flipping through the directory, "Did you hear about the strike? That it's over?"

I told her I had.

She said, "They're tearing down the old apartments on the east side of the park. Did you know that?"

I didn't.

She said, "Those building were old, but they looked so strong, so solid! They're only rubble now. Nothing but rubble." She seemed to be having trouble finding the number she was looking for. She said, as if to herself, "Poor

Mrs Johnson", and then, "You know, I don't think I ever told you this."

She had been shocked, she told me, the first time she saw Mrs Johnson. The poor woman's head moved ceaselessly in every direction. Her tongue hung uncontrollably out of her mouth. She drooled. Her hands, the fingers forced open like claws, were never still. Fiona, then bearing her child, had been moved to pity – for the woman, and for the man who pushed her in the wheelchair, spoke to her and stopped every now and then to wipe the spittle from her chin. But later, whenever she saw the invalid wife of Mr Johnson, she had been unable, she said, to still the jubilation ringing in her heart.

She read American history. She gave up, while she waited to leave the building, her trips to museums and art galleries. Furniture for the new apartment ceased to be important. Beyond the double-locked door, in an apartment flooded with sunlight, the city spread out gloriously below her, she looked at appalling pictures of black men, women and children lined up to be sold like cattle; of a black man hanging from a tree, his head resting unnaturally on his shoulder, his hands tied behind his back, while white men, women and children looked gleefully up at him; of water cannons and lunging, fanged dogs held on long leashes by policemen with drawn revolvers; and of a young black man, his face contorted with rage, frozen in one triumphant second of a crazed dance over the bodies of the black and white policemen he had just killed.

It had seemed to her, she said, that nothing had changed. That the past from which the hanged man and his gleeful spectators had emerged in their antiquated clothes to horrify her was waiting, as Mr Johnson waited for her in the corridor, to surprise and ambush her child in the future. That, not yet out of her uterus, her child was already carrying as its own memory and its own actual experience all that she had read and been horrified by. Then, waiting for its birth, she had thought how cowardly she was because she could not bring herself to abort it, to kill it herself before the Mr Johnsons killed it for her. She had felt so guilty, so responsible, she said, that she wished she could make of the ugly past she read about, and the future she dreaded for her child, her past, the account of the life that she had already lived. She wanted to live and relive it endlessly, again and again, so that her unborn child might not have to, might be spared, because it was innocent and had not asked to be born. She could not carry it, kicking sometimes as if impatient to be born, safe in her womb forever. She had wanted to assume to herself all the lack of worth that others had ascribed to her child in the past and were waiting to ascribe to it in the future. And, because she had been unable to do so, she, without whom it would never have existed, became worthless herself because she would bring it into the world and be unable to protect it.

She had found the number she had been looking for. She was dialling now. I heard her say into the telephone, "Hello? My name is Fiona Lynch. I've killed a man and his wife. I'm at…" and she gave my name and office address.

I waited for her to put the receiver down again, then asked, "Can I get you a cup of coffee?"

She nodded and said, "I've had a very strange day."

CHAPTER FOURTEEN.

She had slipped and fallen in the street. A man had helped her up. When she turned, embarrassed, to thank him, she had found herself face to face with Mr Johnson.

He asked her, kindly, "Are you all right?"

"He had not," Fiona said, a note of wonder in her voice, "recognized me at all!"

Mr Johnson patted her on the shoulder. He said, "There. You should be all right, now."

She had murmured, "Thank you."

"How could I not be civil, too?" she asked me.

"You're welcome," Mr Johnson said. He gave Fiona a business card, "just in case". Then he bowed, touched his hat and walked away.

Her sense of an ambush is deep. She says she feels like the deer in the last book she had been reading with Mike before Tom took him to visit his grandparents in the Caribbean. Stalked by hunters wearing the skins of deer they had previously killed, the frightened deer flare their nostrils, raise their heads, and see only other deer. Fiona, standing as if rooted to the pavement, Mr Johnson having disappeared into the crowd, can see nothing on the busy street to run away from or turn and present a lowered head to.

Her sense of herself as individual is outraged. She is disgusted by the all-else-effacing whiteness Mr Johnson has just conferred upon her. She has, very strongly, a sense of her annihilation. She feels stripped of her past, her formation in Scotland, of everything that made her who she was before she met Mr Johnson. She feels, she tells me, stripped of her very self. It is as if those other selves Mr Johnson had manufactured for her: the nigger-lover and prostitute of the corridor; the white woman he has so courteously helped up from the pavement; and the creature – hardly able to contain her rage and her wonder – whom he is unaware he has just created: it is as if all those manufactured selves can never again come together to form the person she was before she met him.

She feels a hand on her arm, hears a woman's voice say, "Are you all right'?" and is aware that she has been murmuring to herself. "I am," she hears herself say softly to the strange white face looking concernedly at her, "I am, I am, I am." The very words she would scream over Mr Johnson's body after she had shot him.

When she finds the gun in the park, she is sure she has been chosen. The young black man in a grey sweatsuit appearing suddenly around a bend in the path, racing past, then disappearing; the sound of an object falling in the hedge next to her; the two policemen, black and white, appearing for an instant, guns drawn, then disappearing too: everything had seemed providential. Heaven sent. She picks up the gun and puts it in her purse, next to Mr Johnson's card. She has been chosen – by Mr Johnson himself and by the black stranger who has miraculously appeared to hand over his weapon, the instrument of her deliverance.

And when, just before she shoots Mr Johnson, she speaks to him in her Scottish accent and sees on his face, momentarily, before the first bullet hits him and he staggers back, a look of recognition, a memory that went beyond the woman he helped on the street and welcomed into his home, she feels – the smoking gun in her hand – as exultant as a soldier celebrating that she is alive and that it is the body of her enemy that lies in its blood on the elegant Persian carpet. Nor has she been just a soldier. In that large sun-filled room with its glorious view of the city, exactly like the one she has been forced by Mr Johnson to give up, surrounded by his valuable American paintings and sculptures, she has become beyond value herself. She has become a patriot. America is now a better, safer place. Her son and all the other children of America, black and white, are now forever safe from the man whom she has killed.

It is then that she hears the sound, unintelligible, but distinctly human, and turns to the invalid in her wheelchair, jerking even more frantically than usual, and shoots her without anger, but also without compassion. Then she throws away the gun in disgust, opens the door of the apartment and confidently enters the corridor.

I listened to Fiona. I had not been smart enough to think of making Mr Johnson my accomplice in bringing about his own death. He had done it himself. It was he, not I, who had outraged her as an individual; he, not I, who had conferred, in her words, his all-else-effacing whiteness upon her; he, not I, who had made her feel annihilated, stripped of her very self, of everything that had once made her who she was. I was grateful to him for that.

Fiona was saying now that as she walked the street amid the smell of garbage, she had wanted to shout over the whine and jangle of the garbage trucks, jubilantly, for all to hear, that her enemy was dead and she had killed him to prevent him from killing her. Then she had realized that walking with her on the street, keeping pace with her, and unremarked and unremarkable like her, she who had just killed, were all the other Mr Johnsons who had not revealed themselves to her, and that, therefore, she, her child and all the children of America were no safer now than they had been before she murdered Mr Johnson.

She panicked and felt vulnerable. She remembered that the gun – with her fingerprints on it – was on the floor of Mr Johnson's apartment where she had thrown it (in disgust after shooting the invalid); that the doorman, letting her into the apartment building, had recognized and greeted her and said goodbye to her pleasantly as she left; and that the click, which had seemed so much to mark her triumphant entry, unafraid, this time, into the corridor where he had once terrified her, only meant that the door to Mr Johnson's apartment was locked and she could not enter it again.

Walking on the street, still unremarked and unremarkable, she felt herself suddenly watched suspiciously by people to whom she could not explain why she had killed a man who had never laid a hand on her except to help her up after she had fallen. She heard cries of outrage at the murder of the invalid, and saw herself pursued, caught and hung from a tree, her hands tied behind her back, and those same people among whom she was walking, now unremarked and unremarkable, looking gleefully up at her. She decided then to give herself up. That was why, she said, she had come to me.

"I only hope Mike will be safe on that island," she said. I didn't answer, so she continued, "Tom couldn't possibly want to bring him back here. He's too busy with his job to take care of him. Besides, he wouldn't want Mike to live here where his mother is a murderess, don't you think?"

I didn't understand her logic. There were more spouses and offspring of murderers living in America – because there were more murderers in America – than there were living in any other country in the world.

Fiona asked, "Did you know there are snakes on that island?"

I knew. I had been afraid of them myself. Deadly snakes,

called fer-de-lance, not native to the island, had been introduced by slave owners and released into the hills to discourage their property from running away. But I told Fiona I didn't know. I asked her about them.

When she was there, she said, on her way from Edinburgh to America, they had staged a snake and mongoose fight for her. The snake, a full grown adult, had been killed. But, a few days later, a child had been bitten by another snake, a baby, only a few days old, but whose venom was as deadly as an adult's, and the child had died because, on that snake-infested island, the hospital had run out of serum with which to treat it.

"But Mike will be safe there," she said. "Safer than he could ever be in this godforsaken country. Don't you think so?"

I didn't need to think. I knew that he would be. I kept silent.

Fiona said, "I feel so free! So very, very free!"

I felt my old anger and resentment, which I thought I had long ago laid to rest, begin to rise. She was about to be imprisoned for a very long time, perhaps even to be legally killed, and she was talking about being free. I knew what she meant. She had, finally, as I would never be able to, put down her burden of being black in America. She had rid herself of husband and son. She had made herself white again. Whiteness, after all, had not been dispensable for her.

I said enviously, viciously, "You didn't have to kill a white man to get rid of a pair of niggers."

I had taken her by surprise.

She said, "What did you just say?"

I repeated it.

She said, "Don't you dare call my son that." Her eyes were blazing.

I said, "Mr Johnson would have been proud of you.

You've done his dirty work for him. You've reclaimed a nigger-lover. But no matter what you do now, you're still a nigger-lover. You've got a nigger son." Then I added, because I envied her and wanted to hurt her as much as possible, "You're one of us."

"Bastard!" she screamed.

I despised her. Immigrant, like me, she was the immigrant to America that I could never be. I began to call her softly, with deep satisfaction, all the insulting names for white in America that I had made it my business to learn and had been careful, before now, not openly to use. Every time she tried to speak, I raised my voice above hers. Watching with pleasure her indignant, reddened face, I repeated the demeaning names. I became transported, lost in the sudden joy of my unexpected outburst, as though, throughout my life in America, I had been building all along, unknowingly, towards this moment of liberating outpouring.

When, finally, I stopped, Fiona exploded. She stood up. She raised her voice over mine and called me nigger. She called me spook. She called me coon. She called me nap, satchel-mouth, jigaboo. She called me ape. She called me other names, many, many other names. She described me angrily in our country's terms, using words to name me that I had learned long ago and had forgotten. I recognized a fellow scholar. I acknowledged her obsession. She, too, had felt impelled to dig out and become familiar with all the names that existed in our country for me and for her husband and for her child. I understood, more than from anything she had told me before, the depths of her anxiety. She had even, this gentile, this shiksa, called me *schwartzer*. She stopped screaming and sat down and put her hands to her face. I watched her breathe deeply in and out a few times. I heard her say, "My God! Oh, my God!"

I felt the gooseflesh on my skin as if each pore was an

outlet for Fiona's anguish. But I refused to permit myself to feel sorry for her. I went into the reception room. I didn't want to look upon her desperation anymore. Jennifer looked interrogatively up at me. I told her only that she could leave, that I would close up. When the police arrived, I told them where Fiona was. Without a word to her, I watched them lead her away. But, I decided, I would not send her a bill for this visit.

The telephone rang. But it wasn't Peggy. It was Paul. He wanted to drive with me tomorrow to C.B.'s funeral. After I hung up, I closed the office and went outside where Franz was waiting to drive me home for the last time.

PART THREE

CHAPTER FIFTEEN

That night, for the first time in years, I dreamt of Beatrice. I was sleeping on a bed next to her and birds, singing in the mango tree in the yard, laden with ripe fruit, had awakened me. In the dream, I lay contentedly next to her and listened to the birds. The smell of ripe mangoes and of Beatrice was as comforting as a childhood memory. But I had never slept in a house with a mango tree in its backyard and had never awakened, in a bed or anywhere else, to find Beatrice next to me. Now, I awoke in my high-rise apartment, my eyes still closed, the sounds and scents of my dream all about me. I heard myself breathing deeply, evenly. Gradually, the singing of the birds and the nostalgic smell of mangoes and of Beatrice, as I had learned to know it the last time I was on her island, disappeared. Now I heard only the steady, quietly efficient, mechanical throbbing – louder now than the beating of my heart – of the apartment building. I reluctantly opened my eyes. I thought of calling Peggy, but it was nine o'clock, only six in California, and I didn't want to wake her. Besides, it was time to get ready for Red's funeral.

But as I stood under the jet of water and adjusted it, I found myself thinking of Craig, the fellow student Peggy had been in love with at Berkeley, who was now a professor of music at Stanford. I saw his white face, which Peggy's parents had objected to, lying on a pillow next to hers, his arm thrown, as I had sometimes awakened to find my own, across her naked body. My eyes were closed. The water was deliciously warm on my body. There was no steam in the room. The efficient fan made it as comfortable as though I were bathing outside on a Caribbean island. But I felt threatened by that recumbent and proprietary arm I had imagined. It lay beyond the capacity of my wealth and my professional reputation to protect me from my jealousy.

I chided myself. Peggy had postponed our marriage until after her parents were dead, because she didn't want to hurt them, but she never ceased to tell me how handsome I was. But, the next moment, I had replaced Craig with someone else, this time wholly of my imagination – a Japanese-American like herself, a man, that is, of her own kind, whom her parents knew instinctively was more suitable than I as a lover and husband. His black moustache stood out, well-trimmed, against his skin. He was lithe, small-boned, muscular. His strong fingers, karate-trained, caressed Peggy's straight oriental pubic hair authoritatively, without racial diffidence, until she began to move in the way I knew so well…

The doorbell rang. I opened my eyes. I turned off the shower and stood before the mirror. I looked at my reflection as I dried myself – my flared nose, thick lips, short curly hair encroaching low on my narrow forehead. Peggy, playfully refusing me, often sent me off to find Masai maidens and long-legged Caucasian models. She would ask, laughing, "What do you see in a short little Jap like me?"

I put on my robe and went to open the door for Paul. He was carrying a large cardboard box in both hands and, under an arm, in its case, was his flute. I remembered. It was Halloween. There were costumes in that box, fifteen small, satiny colourful costumes with wire-stiff tails, depicting rats and a large one for the Pied Piper of Hamelin. But, as he entered the apartment and set the box down on the floor, Paul, in his black mourning suit, looked a very sad Piper-to-be.

We shook hands. He wanted coffee and went into the kitchen to make some for us. I could see he was in no mood to talk. Selwyn had told me of Paul's attempts to meet with Red. During every one of his first few years in America, he had given a free concert in the ghetto. He put up huge posters bearing his picture and his name. The posters were intended to work like magnets. They were to draw Red out from his hiding place in the ghetto. But the posters, Selwyn said, had not worked. Red had never once shown up. So, after three or four years, Paul had given up his concerts and had substituted his annual Halloween excursions for them.

A little later, from my bedroom, I heard him playing his flute. But the mournful tune sounded more like a farewell to Red, about to depart permanently from the ghetto, than like the attractive melody that could tempt fifteen costumed youngsters out of it, for one night, to follow Paul from luxurious apartment to luxurious apartment, in the prestigious neighbourhood where he and I lived.

The music stopped. Paul entered the bedroom with two cups of coffee and placed one on the dresser before which I was standing, putting on my tie. I watched him in the mirror, sitting on the edge of the bed, looking at the cup of coffee on the floor at his feet and hitting the open palm of one hand listlessly with the white gloves he held in the other.

I said, "Franz and I split. He's not going to be my chauffeur anymore." And I told him about Franz's offer of a replacement.

Paul stopped hitting his palm with the gloves, became serious, watched my reflection looking in the mirror at him and said, "So what're you going to do about the man you couldn't do without?"

"Franz has very good judgement," I said. I trust him. If he says the man is good, I'm sure he'll be."

Paul said, "You know, of course, what that man will be."

"Very good. I'm sure of it."

"And black."

One Sunday, a couple of years before, Franz had driven me to Paul's for brunch and we had seen Paul, carrying two full grocery bags, about to enter his building.

Franz must have read the review of Paul's concert performance the night before. He said to him, "Mr Paul, you and the Doc here are a real credit to your race. Your people must be really proud of you."

Paul smiled and did not answer him. But when he and I were waiting in the lobby for the elevator, he said, "The next time I'll ask your man to tell me what my race is. He seems to know."

Now, putting on my coat, I said to Paul, "It doesn't matter, does it? So long as the man is courteous, respectful and a good driver. Does it?"

Paul said, "That's not the point…"

But he didn't say any more. The buzzer sounded. The doorman announced that the driver was in the lobby.

"Ready?" I asked Paul.

He nodded. We descended to the lobby. And Paul was right. The man Franz had replaced himself with was a black man.

CHAPTER SIXTEEN

His name was Roscoe. Sitting with Paul in the back of the car, it was strange, after the years of looking at Franz's thick mane, to be looking at the short, spring-coiled, grey and white hair above Roscoe's broad neck. I remembered my father.

On Saturdays, I used to drive with him along the unfamiliarly steep, curving roads on Beatrice's island where he was the new magistrate. My father, concentrating, driving his new car inexpertly, made me sit in the back seat and hardly spoke to me. I looked at the lush, precipitous drops below the winding road, so different from the bare, limestone features of my native island, and, every now and then, at the short black-and-white hair coiled like miniature springs at the back of my father's head.

We had been living on the island barely a year. The small Protestant community, eager for recruits, especially prominent recruits such as someone in my father's official position, had embraced us. There had been parties, announcements, introductions and presentations at church. There was the large government-owned house on the peninsula overlooking the harbour. And there was the new car, my father's first. The long years of study by correspondence courses – while he worked his way up from elementary school teacher, himself just out of elementary school, to headmaster and village elderman, then to university graduate and, finally, holder of a law degree – that long journey – had paid off. But my father wasn't satisfied. He had already started work, through more correspondence courses, on a master's degree in Law.

I was sick in bed with chicken pox on the Saturday during the rainy season when they found him with a broken neck in his car, in one of the deep ravines below the road. I turned away from Roscoe's neck and, through the window, saw the garbage piled high on either side of the street. Soon, we were in front of the funeral home. There was garbage on the pavement on both sides of it, but the pavement in front of it was clean. Selwyn and a white man were standing and talking to each other on the pavement.

Paul and I greeted Selwyn and nodded to the stranger. Selwyn was chuckling and watching Paul and me closely. He made no attempt to introduce the stranger. The stranger smiled, held out his hand to Paul and me in turn, and greeted us by name. His accent was American. I was surprised how comfortable he looked, standing with us on the ghetto pavement. Selwyn began to laugh.

The stranger said, "My name is Olsen. Frederick Olsen. Babsy is my mother."

Babsy was an island name! I looked carefully at the stranger. Selwyn was laughing.

Paul said excitedly, in his island accent which he, alone of the four of us, still used, "You're Bam. Red Bam!"

His accent burst like a sudden, unexpected light upon the moment of my recognition. My face became tight with embarrassment. Frederick's father, I thought, would have needed to be a Scandinavian giant. For the Babsy I remembered, the mother of Red Bam, was short, Indian, a prostitute who catered only to the white sailors of ships calling into the island's harbour. When the ships were in, she put on shoes and walked on the arm of her sailor escort. Her black, straight hair hung down to her waist. A cigarette swung in her hand as she walked. She wore a flower in her hair. Her lips were red. There was rouge on her cheeks. Striding along the street, she seemed to care nothing for those who, like my mother, watched from behind their jalousies and judged her. After my father's death, when we could no longer afford a servant and I was busy preparing for the scholarship examination, her son ran errands for us. He cleaned the yard on Saturdays. My mother gave him lunch. While she and I sat on the table in the dining room and ate off the bone china my father had brought from England (she had not yet sold it), Red Bam sat on the step and ate with his fingers out of an enamel plate. My mother forbade me to play with him. He did not attend school, frequented the wharf, was an excellent swimmer. He guided Canadian and American sailors about the town and carried their packages for them. He cleaned the decks of their yachts and ate and drank aboard ship with them. When the yachts and yachtsmen were not in, I used to watch him walk the streets nearly always by himself or with one or two of those whom we called, scornfully, wharf rats, who were the only friends he seemed to have, and whose ridicule and derision he had often to endure. After my father's death, studying furiously for the scholarship that would enable me to leave the island, I used to pretend that I was as isolated on it as he was. One day, he disappeared. We heard that a couple had taken him away with them on their yacht. Long before any other of us, Red Bam had come to America to be transformed.

Selwyn was enjoying the surprise he had sprung upon us. Paul was obviously delighted to see Frederick Olsen. While Paul asked questions, I looked at Frederick. He seemed to have no memory of the past I remembered, nor of Red Bam, son of the disdained and even more disdaining Indian prostitute, who stood out among us not so much because of his appearance as because of the information we possessed about his origins. Frederick Olsen, standing comfortably with Paul and Selwyn and myself in the American ghetto, waiting to say goodbye to Red, whom he could not have known, though he obviously remembered C.B., behaved as if he had always been one of us. And none of us, it seemed to me, was going to evoke the past as accurately as I remembered it.

Selwyn said, "I haven't seen this man since he was twelve years old."

Paul asked, "How's your mother?"

Frederick, smiling, said, "She's fine."

I asked, "Where have you been all these years?"

He said, "In the States. Right here, man." He seemed happy to say it, and seemed to want to sound less American than when he first spoke.

No one asked about the name, Frederick Olsen. On the island, he had not seemed to need a name. We all knew him as Red Bam who was different from the derelict, older Black Bam, who had not had a sailor for a father and who was dying, in front of the rum shops, of a gangrenous leg wrapped in a dirty bandage.

The last time I had been on the island, I saw Babsy often. She worked as a janitor and domestic servant who cleaned Beatrice's hairdressing salon. The long hair of her once proudly held, contemptuous head was cut short and streaked with grey. Her bare feet had blackened slits on their thick, calloused sides. Every evening, from Beatrice's verandah, I watched this once proud woman, rendered contemptuous by the contempt of others, go piously to Vespers and Benediction in the Roman Catholic cathedral across the street.

"She's rich," Beatrice told me once, "don't mind that you see her looking so down-and-out. Someone's sending her money every month, they say. She doesn't touch it. It's all in the bank. They say it's one of her ex-sailors who can't forget her." Beatrice laughed. "You know how they gossip here!"

None of that seemed to matter now. Babsy's son was in the shipping business. He gave each of us a card: FREDERICK OLSEN ENTERPRISES, INC. SHIPPING. MIAMI, NEW YORK, SAN FRANCISCO. He showed us pictures. He said, "That's Karen, she's my wife." A blonde, half-torso, smiling between two young girls. "That's Barbara and that's Betsy."

I noticed the B's. He was loyal to Babsy. The others, I am sure, noticed that, too. But no one commented on this. The door of the funeral parlour opened and a man, dressed in black, motioned us in. I gave the family pictures back to Frederick and followed the others inside.

I looked at the body lying in the coffin. I tried to imagine that I was looking at the man who used to be my best friend. I felt I was confronting a stranger. Selwyn had said that Red had been shot in the forehead. I tried to find the bullet holes and, when I couldn't, raised my eyes and saw Frederick Olsen standing on the other side of the coffin across from me. His head was bowed, his eyes were closed, his cheeks red with obvious emotion. He took a kerchief from his pocket and held it to his moist eyes. Then he raised his head, saw me looking at him and, as if embarrassed, bowed his head quickly again.

But I had seen his grief. Its genuineness moved me. I looked down again at the body in the coffin and, my head bowed, my eyes rolled tensely upward. I watched Frederick. He had not known Red. He and C.B. could never have been friends on the island. I was impressed that he should so grieve, standing unselfconsciously with us in the funeral home of an American ghetto, for a man with whom all he shared was an accidental birth on a small Caribbean island. I felt rebuked by his grief. And I allowed myself to feel a retaliatory spasm – a sharp, painful sting – of resentment towards him. He, I thought, alone of all of us, might be said to have truly come home to America, to have properly inherited, in America, his father's patrimony, no matter where in the world his father, the unknown white sailor who did not even know he had sired him, had actually come from.

My eyes, straining upwards to watch him enviously, with a resentment I did not want to feel, were getting tired. I turned them fully on the figure in the coffin. I pretended I was beginning to see, in the face of the dead man, some traces of the angry, hurt and non-conforming C.B. whom I remembered and wanted, guiltily now, to say goodbye to. But it was my past, I realized, that I wanted to say goodbye to. I felt ashamed, deeply ashamed, of my resentment of Frederick. I apologized silently to him. And to C.B.. I acknowledged Red. I said goodbye to both and, bowed over their body in the coffin, said goodbye, too, to Beatrice and to all her surrogates who had not even resembled her. I closed my eyes, said goodbye to my past and prayed for a new, for another, life.

I wanted another life. I was tired of fighting, tired of being a warrior and guerilla. I was ready to sue for peace with myself, with my past and with my country and my country-men. I wanted to live in America with Peggy as once I had imagined I could live in the Caribbean with Beatrice. I wanted to be happy, to make Peggy happy. I wanted her to nurse me out of my past as if I were one of those sea birds she had told me about on the California sand, who did not proclaim their distress until you came close to them. From a distance, the afflicted bird looked healthy and ready to fly away if you came too close. But Peggy approached and it did not fly. She saw tar on its wings and feet. She saw its distress. She picked up the creature, took it home. One day, she watched it take wing and soar, healthy again, into the sky.

Let her disapproving parents die quickly, I prayed over the body in the coffin, so that I could marry her.

I raised my head from my communion with Red, my fellow American, opened my eyes, and saw that the others had left the room. I kissed the cold forehead. I asked forgiveness of C.B., my fellow islander, who was once my best friend. Then I left them both.

Outside, I said goodbye cordially to Frederick who had an important business meeting in Florida and would not be going to the cemetery. I felt, now, not the slightest resentment towards him. We had not made the world, he and I. We merely lived in a world that others, more powerful than we, had arranged for us. I gave him my address and telephone number and told him, genuinely, that I hoped to see him again soon. Selwyn got into his rented car, which he would drive directly to the airport from the cemetery. Paul and I headed to where Roscoe was waiting for us in Franz's taxi.

And the two cars followed the hearse slowly out of the neighbourhood that the rest of us had avoided and that Red would never again return to.

CHAPTER SEVENTEEN

When we returned to my apartment after the burial, Paul went straight to the spare bedroom to rest before his night's work as the Pied Piper of the ghetto. Peggy, finally, had called. Jennifer said that she was arriving at the airport at three p.m. It was one o'clock. I told Jennifer to cancel my appointments for the rest of the day, then threw myself, fully dressed, across the bed.

Soon I am walking alone on the otherwise empty street in the city early on a Sunday morning. It is summer. Out of a cloudless sky, a rising sun lights up the tallest skyscrapers on one side of the street above the shadows cast upon them by the buildings on the other side. Down on the pavement it is cool and still early-morning-pleasant. Suddenly, a taxi appears and pulls up beside me. Franz is at the wheel. He is smiling; I am delighted to see him again. The back door of the taxi opens and Ekua emerges from it.

She is superb – tall, loose-limbed, beautifully angular. Her hair is cropped short. A blue-and-white patterned cloth is wrapped about her. She looks vital, loved, taken care of. Laughing, she gives me the bundle she is carrying in both hands.

"This is for you," she says.

I open the bundle and look upon our son for the first time.

Ekua says, "Kiss me. Kiss me."

I want to make love to her. I want to possess, to own her. I kiss her chastely on the cheek. She laughs and says, "I've been having such a good time! There's no time that my friends want me that I am not at home for them."

I am dismayed. I have a picture of a house full of people, and of fun and pleasure from which I am excluded. I want desperately not to be.

Then Ekua says, laughing still, "My house burnt down," and I am relieved. There is now no place for her to be happy without me. I look closely at her face. I want to see on it that she is sad telling me how happy she is. I want to see that the story of her happiness without me is untrue. I look for tears behind her smile. But there are no tears on that radiant face. And I am overwhelmed by what I have lost and because she is happy without me.

Then, abruptly, I am alone with Franz and he is driving me along the unpaved main street of Ekua's village. The one she had so often described to me in England. Franz has been transformed. He is a West African now. He's driving me to see Ekua, but he doesn't know who I am. He doesn't know that I know Ekua. It is no longer Sunday or morning. I no longer know what day of the week it is. The sun is about to set and on the single dirt road without lights, which Ekua had told me about, it will soon be dark.

Franz, my West African driver, says, "I used to like her. She was so beautiful! But she became cheap. She married a foreigner."

He uses the word for foreigner that Ekua had taught me, in London, which also means European or white man. Suddenly, we are no longer in the car and Franz, the West African, is patting me on the back with a closed fist. I become suspicious. I force open his hand and discover a knife. He has been stabbing me with it. I feel nothing and

118

there's no blood. I take the knife away from him. While I am doing so, Ekua reappears and says happily, "You lost out. You lost out. My American friend is so handsome! Broad-shouldered and narrow-hipped!" I am dismayed again. Franz has disappeared and I am alone with her.

I awoke. The bedroom was full of the flavour of Ekua. Every breath I drew seemed to carry her scent. But "broad-shouldered" and "narrow-hipped" were words Peggy sometimes used to describe me. I opened my eyes and saw that it was time to collect her. Paul was still asleep. I left him a note saying I had gone to the airport.

When Peggy emerged with the other passengers, I rushed to wrap my arms about her. I said, "I missed you so! Don't ever leave me again."

She stood on the tips of her toes to kiss me.

"I won't."

I said, "Are you hungry? Are you tired? Have you eaten? You didn't call."

She put a finger on my lips. "Don't fuss." She wasn't tired. She wasn't hungry. She had eaten on the plane.

"Will you spend the night...?"

"Of course," she said. Then, "I have good news. We've been nominated for the National Book Award. I'm excited. I think we stand a chance."

"We?"

"I couldn't have written it without his collaboration." She rose on her toes and pecked me on the cheek. "Nor yours. Thanks."

I said, "I left him sleeping in the apartment. We buried Red today. Remember him?"

She said, "Of course. Beatrice's brother. The friend I never could get to talk to. What happened?"

"He was shot."

"Yeah." She said it as if the news of Red's death was

inevitable and she had been waiting for it. I told her about Frederick Olsen and, later, when we came to the taxi and she saw Roscoe behind the wheel, I told her about my quarrel with Franz.

When we got to my apartment, Paul had already left with his box of costumes and his flute. I offered Peggy a glass of her favourite wine from California. I put on her favourite among Paul's performances, that of Beethoven's violin concerto. I had all the ingredients to prepare her favourite Japanese dish had she been hungry. I had been ready for days to welcome her back.

The American accent that I heard as I approached Paul's dressing room nearly three years ago had not prepared me for the short, Asian woman who greeted me. Paul had said only that a woman was writing his biography and wanted to speak to as many of his boyhood friends as she could.

I had concealed my surprise that someone who looked like her should speak the way she did. At dinner, I watched, and listened fascinatedly to her. I could not get over how completely American she sounded. Once, I put my hands surreptitiously over my ears. The face I looked at, its mouth opening and closing suddenly, was just another oriental face. I uncovered my ears. The American accent conferred mystery and magic upon that oriental face. I still think of Peggy as exotic, strange and wondrous. After nearly four years!

I smiled contentedly at her.

She said, "What's funny?"

"You are."

Then I asked, "How's Craig?"

Peggy laughed. "How's Craig? How's Craig? Darling, you're too old to be jealous." She didn't know how Craig was. She hadn't seen him. He wasn't in California while she was there.

She had removed her dress and her shoes. Beneath her full slip, I saw her bra and her underpants. She looked fragile. But I knew how tough she was, except with regard to dealing with her parents' wishes concerning her marriage. She removed a clown's costume from her suitcase and gave it to me.

"You deserve this. You've earned it by being jealous. I'm taking you to a party tonight."

Once, before she told me the reason why she could not marry me, when she still used to send me, laughingly, off to Masai maidens or long-legged Caucasian models, or ask playfully what I saw in a short, little Jap like her, she said – rejecting me yet another time – "Let's not have any Jiggers yet. Let's not add to America's vocabulary."

"Jiggers?"

"Yes. Jiggers. The children of Japs and niggers." And she burst out laughing.

When she finally told me about Craig and herself and explained that she did not wish to displease her parents who were old and would die soon, and would prefer to wait until they were dead before she married me, I could not be angry. But I was always very careful not to ask her how her parents were.

CHAPTER EIGHTEEN

That night, she and I were standing at a street corner trying to get a taxi. The street was crowded with devils, imps, goblins and hobgoblins, and all other kinds of dangerous Halloween creatures – masked and unmasked – who were fortunate enough not yet to have bitten on a razor blade embedded in an apple, or to have chewed on finely ground glass mixed in with powdered candy.

Peggy, under her coat, was dressed in Arabian Nights silk. Orange trousers, tight at the ankles, were full about her slightly bowed legs. Her green bodice, closed at the throat, was full-sleeved and undulant. Her shoes, golden and turned up at the toes, were like fragile miniature canoes. Her mask and gloves, like mine, were in her handbag. Beneath my unbuttoned overcoat, I was wearing the clown's costume she had brought me.

There was a newspaper booth at the corner. The vendor was happily giving candy to the creatures who dared him. He told me how well I looked. I said, "You haven't seen all of it." I asked Peggy for my mask and put it on. The vendor laughed. He said, "That's even better."

I could see the headline of one of his papers: SUCCESSFUL IMMIGRANT AND PROMINENT ART DEALER AND INVALID WIFE KILLED.

There was a large picture of my fellow immigrant, Mr

Johnson, a kind-looking, late middle-aged man whom, had I been white, I would have been pleased to call "Father". Then, in the masthead, I saw the small picture of Jonathan and, next to it, the words: IMPORTANT NEW AMERICAN NOVEL, p. 33.

I was about to ask the vendor for a paper when I felt a tap on my shoulder and turned. The face I looked at, on a level with my own, was swathed in bandages. Only the eyes, flared nostrils and the thick lips showed. There was a bulge on one side of the bandaged head. Between the open sides of the camel hair overcoat, I saw the colourful silk tie on the elegant shirt front.

I said, my voice distorted by my mask, "Nice disguise, Walker."

"You're not bad yourself, Doc."

"How did you recognize me?" I asked.

"I saw you from across the street. I saw you put your mask on."

I took my mask and gave it back to Peggy. I introduced her to Walker. He shook her hand and said to me, "God takes care of babes and fools. He sure took care of you."

I struck him playfully on the side of the head.

Walker cried out and staggered back. Peggy, the vendor and I laughed. But there were tears in Walker's eyes. The bandage had turned red where I had struck him. I said, "Is that ketchup or tomato sauce?"

Walker put a hand gingerly to the red spot on his bandaged face. He said, "You hurt me, Doc. That's blood. Real blood. That's no fake. You hurt just like the rest of 'em."

I laughed and said with mock concern, "I'm sorry," and pretended I was about to hit him again. He jumped back. He seemed afraid I might actually harm him. He was always a good actor.

"Oh no, you don't, Doc. Once is enough."

I laughed.

A taxi, flagged by Peggy, had come to a squealing stop at the curb next to us.

I said to Walker, "We're going downtown. Need a ride?"

"Why not? Might as well."

Two blocks into our ride I knew why he had so readily accepted my offer. He pointed to his bandaged head and said, "Want to hear about this?"

I didn't. I wasn't ready for another of his stories. But Peggy was. She said enthusiastically, "Yes. Please tell us."

Walker told us how he was on a cross-town bus on his way to a memorial service in a synagogue when he saw a man with a camera taking pictures of him. He looked up at the man who was now aiming the camera everywhere on the bus except at Walker. Walker became suspicious.

He says, "A fat white guy with a beard and wearing sunglasses in a bus? You gotta be suspicious. Especially when he's taking your picture and pretending he isn't."

Walker told us he took out his own sunglasses and put them on. He picked up the sports page from the empty seat next to him and pretended to read it. He fixed his eyes, behind his sunglasses, on the photographer. Before long, he saw the camera aimed at him. He saw it steady. He heard the click. He looked up. The man was aiming the camera here, there, and everywhere – except at him.

Walker got up from his aisle seat near the middle of the bus and walked towards the front where the man was standing, his back against a metal pole.

"Were you taking my picture?" he asked.

The man paid no attention. Walker asked again, "Did you just take my picture?"

This time the man looked at him. But he still didn't answer.

Walker tells us, "The guy wasn't deaf or dumb. He'd

come on the bus with another man, a cripple with a yarmulke, and a huge bag on his shoulder. They were talking to each other. The cripple was walking as if he had no toes…" As soon as I hear Walker say that I know why his story sounds familiar. I think: Walker has finally become mad. He has become a character in a novel. I keep quiet. Walker isn't my patient now.

He says, "I point to the guy's Minox. I say, 'You take my picture. I no give permission. Why you do so?' The guy may be a tourist. Perhaps he doesn't speak English. I don't want to upset him. I only want to know why he's taking my picture and pretends he's not. But the guy is no tourist. He is as American as you and me, Doc. He says, 'Don't be a smartass. You know why.' I tell him, 'I don't. And you better fucking well tell me.' He shouts, 'Because you're a thief! A fucking pickpocket! That's why.'"

Walker pauses. He has already strayed from the original story. I'm interested in his version. He begins to laugh. I know why. In the original, the pickpocket follows the photographer's uncle into the lobby of his apartment building and tries to frighten the old man by showing him his penis. I wait. Next to me, Walker is almost beside himself with laughter. He says, "You know I'm circumcised. Right, Doc? I told you so."

He had told me. But I wouldn't know until I saw his penis. I could take his word alone for nothing.

He adds, "And I have a small dick. I never told you, because I was afraid you'd laugh at me. Everyone else who saw it did."

I'm still waiting. Walker doesn't seem able now to contain his laughter. He says, as much as it permits him to, "That man was a poet, a fucking genius with words. He made my small black mushroom of a prick a thing of beauty. A large tan-and-purple…"

"…uncircumcised thing," I recite silently along with Walker, "a tube, a snake; metallic hairs…" But Walker is not quoting verbatim. "…a tube," he says. "It hung over my great oval testicles; metallic hairs bristled at its thick base and the tip curled with the fleshly mobility of an elephant's trunk."

He stops. He has left out parts of the original passage which I had once made it my business to memorize. He has left out the iridescent skin, the disappointed expectation that the black skin should be thick or rough. But his version is good enough. Peggy, who has little time for novels, and has missed more than she knows, bursts out laughing. I see that the taxi-driver, protected from us by his bullet-proof glass, is enjoying himself, too. Walker is clapping his hands and bouncing up and down on the car seat. With his bandaged head, he looks like a mummy brought to life again. He says, "All my life I've dreamed of owning a prick like that!"

He decided, Walker says, to enjoy the wonderful instrument the photographer has given him and began to laugh along with the other passengers on the bus. Then he notices that the cripple is not laughing.

I listen to Walker more attentively now. This is all new. This is nothing I remember having read. This is now Walker's story. He says, "I began to think. I asked myself why the cripple wasn't laughing. Everyone else was. I thought it was because he was a cripple and was afraid that if he laughed at me, others could laugh at him. I imagined that everyone on the bus who was laughing knew how small my prick really was. And I became ashamed, as if they'd been ridiculing me all the time."

He pauses. How good he is, I think. Typical Walker. Only he would think of identifying himself with that insulting and dangerous caricature, that criminal and buffoon, civilized – false-frontedly – only in his extraordinarily elegant appearance, who preyed on those least able to defend themselves – weak old men, their poor eyes watering with terror, mouths open with false teeth dropping from the upper gums – who were too foolish to understand that the abnormal thing he carried for a penis was not a gun. But the story is Walker's now. I no longer can recite silently along with him. I can only listen.

He says, "That son of a bitch was holding the camera above his head like a priest before a fucking altar. He had called me uncircumcised. I don't know whether he was circumcised or not. I couldn't tell, anymore than I could tell if his listeners were. But he had boarded the bus with the cripple. I knew only that the cripple and I were circumcised and that everyone else on the bus, circumcised or not, was laughing at me."

At that point, Walker says, he wanted only to get off the damn bus. He realized that he had gone past his stop and has missed the memorial service. The synagogue was several long blocks behind him. He felt like a fool, Walker says, who has been busy laughing only at himself. The photographer was still holding the camera above his head as if it was the Holy Eucharist. All Walker could think of was to take it away from him.

Walker, with us, is no longer laughing. He says, "I wanted to fuck his mother, his wife and his sister with that monstrous tool he had given me. I wanted to hold up his uncle with a fucking gun, not any goddamned prick. I wanted to protect myself somehow. But I was too ashamed to let those on the bus see how small my penis really was. I thought, take the Minox from him, take it from him and break it up. Then perhaps the people might forget what he told them about me. I thought I was going mad with embarrassment."

Walker says he took off his sunglasses, and saw that the

man's eyes, behind his own sunglasses, were closed. Walker grabbed for the Minox. The photographer would not give it up. He and Walker began to fight for it.

The other passengers screamed. The driver stopped the bus. He opened the front doors and Walker and the photographer tumbled onto the street. Walker was holding the photographer by the neck against the front of the bus, and struggling to take the camera away from him. He heard an old male voice say something in a language he didn't understand. He turned and saw an old man, elegantly dressed in an old-fashioned way. He turned back to the photographer. From the other side, he heard a younger, more vigorous voice speaking the same language. He was turning, still holding the photographer by the throat against the front of the bus, to see the owner of this new, soft-spoken voice when, Walker says, the world fell on the side of his face.

He laughs again now, a quieter laugh. He says, seated between Peggy and me, "It wasn't the world at all. It was the goddamn baize bag that had hit me."

Walker began to fall. He saw the cripple smiling and winding up to hit him again. The cripple struck. Walker fell to the ground. There was a terrible roar in his ears, as if the world was grinding to a stop and, above the roar, he heard faintly the voices of the old man and the mad man who had all but killed him, talking in their strange language to each other.

Walker stops. I almost jump out of my seat and shout, "Bravo!"

Peggy says, "How awful!"

I want to tell her that it is only a story, that Walker stole the incident from a novel. I want to say it's only words but that Walker, foolishly, thinks he can become important by pretending that what the words describe actually happened to him. I want to say that it is his way of drawing attention to himself, to tell Peggy that she could not trust people like Walker. He was a fantasist, a fabulator, a mythomaniac. He did not deal with reality. Only in it. And I want to warn her not to waste her time or her sympathy on paranoiacs and hysterics, people who believed they were victims or heroes or martyrs, attention-craving people who did not themselves believe the lies they told. I want to say to Peggy that, in his own way, Walker was a photographer, too; a skilful exploiter of every background, a strategist and chameleon, a master of camouflage, a perpetual convert. He was my patient, I want to tell Peggy, but even I couldn't say who Walker was.

I say none of this. Besides, Walker has not yet finished his story. His assailants, the photographer and the old man, had visited him in the hospital. They brought him flowers and an apology. They had made a mistake. He was not the man the photographer thought he was.

"I accepted the flowers and the apology," he tells Peggy and me. "I couldn't do anything else. I was stoned from all those painkillers. I shook their hands. Even the hands of the mad man who had almost killed me. He was an Israeli from Eastern Europe. He wanted to immigrate, to become American. I saw how big his arms and shoulders were and knew I was lucky to be still alive. I'm not angry. We all do what we have to do to get on."

He pauses. He begins again to chuckle, then openly to laugh. He says, "But you know what? I'll sue the sons of bitches."

He looks with mock suspicion at me. He asks, "You're sure you aren't in the habit of riding that bus, Doc? Don't you need a doctor's touch to be a good pickpocket?"

I laugh. Like me, he really has forgotten nothing of that book. Peggy asks the driver to stop the taxi. We are near her friend's house. She puts on her mask and her gloves. She does not want to risk being recognized. I put on my mask and my gloves, too. The three of us get out of the taxi. The driver says he almost doesn't want to take the tip, he's enjoyed himself so much! He takes it anyway. Peggy and I say goodbye to Walker and the two of us walk to the party, indistinguishable, beneath our costumes, from any other masked and costumed American.

"Poor Walker," Peggy says, "It can't be true, can it?"

I don't answer. I remember Jonathan's picture in the papers. I had been about to buy the paper when Walker interrupted me. I make a note to get a copy of Jonathan's novel as soon as possible.

We climb up the stairs of the brownstone where Peggy's friend lives. I knock on the door. It opens, and the sound of people enjoying themselves is loud. A masked and costumed person at the door motions us in. Without a word, so as not to give herself away, Peggy enters the house. I follow her.

CHAPTER NINETEEN

At first, everyone else at the party had tried to conceal his or her identity from the others. Everyone spoke in a disguised voice, used unself-revealing gestures and assumed postures they normally did not assume. Everyone was overjoyed when one uncovered another. An unselfconscious laugh, an exclamation in a carelessly familiar or no longer sufficiently disguised voice; an involuntary gesture, well known to friends, gave one away. Someone else named him or her excitedly, in a normal voice, and was, in turn, hilariously recognized. I had the pleasant impression that I was on stage among actors in a play. I was not myself an actor. I was neither of the discovered nor of the discoverers. I could not be recognized by anyone other than Peggy. I had no need, behind my mask, further to disguise myself. I spoke in my own voice, used my natural gestures, carried myself as I usually did. The party went on and people gradually forgot their posturings and began more and more to enjoy themselves. I could only pretend that I enjoyed the unwitting self-revelations as much as the others. And though, in the end, I too was discovered, it was only because everyone, having recognized everyone else but me, knew that I had to be Peggy's friend. I took off the mask then.

Now, the party was over and Peggy and I were on the streets again. She said she didn't want to take a taxi. She wanted to walk, at least for part of the way. The early morning air was cool on my face. The unfamiliar taste of bourbon lingered pleasantly on my tongue. The goblins, imps and other magical creatures had disappeared from the streets. The nearly empty pavement did not seem menacing. The few people we passed – couples, costumed and unmasked like us; a small group of costumed revellers, unmasked, too; a solitary drunk now and then – seemed too ordinary to be dangerous. On the street, the cars and trucks and buses, following their headlights, seemed to be apart, in a world of their own. But at a corner newsstand, near which we were waiting for the light to change, the headlines screamed at me that another foolhardy white had been killed in the ghetto.

I suggested the taxi again to Peggy. She had not seen the headlines. She said she wanted to walk. I suggested that we pay Paul a visit and give him the news about her book. When she said yes, I suggested the taxi again. I did not think she could possible want to walk the several blocks to Paul's home near the Cultural Center. But she did. I put myself in her hands. I was in a good mood. I had laughed a lot at the party. I was tipsy. I was having a good time.

We reached the Cultural Center and took a short cut through it to Paul's apartment building. The large concrete plaza, which I usually saw full of visitors during the day, or lit up and full of concert or theatregoers at night, was dimly lit and empty now. Its water-fountain was quiet. Our footsteps on the pavement were loud. I felt safe and comfortable. I put an arm about Peggy's shoulders. We neared the centre of the plaza. The hum of the cars and trucks, cut off partly by the buildings, and gradually diminishing, seemed very far away. Above the distant hum, we began to hear the sounds of skates on concrete. These became louder and louder as we approached the concert hall, and we saw three figures skating ahead of us under one of the far-spaced electric lampposts.

They were masked, and dressed like clowns. One had a jester's cap on. Another was a harlequin. The third wore a costume like mine and his mask was exactly like the one I had left behind at the party. I became uneasy. But the skaters paid no attention to us. The one wearing the jester's cap had skates on his hands as well as on his feet. He skated on his feet. He skated on his hands, his feet in the air. He brought his feet down again and skated, his back to the sky, on hands and feet, on feet and one hand, and on hands and one foot. He skated again on all fours, then raised his upper body upright and, without a pause and skating all the time, bent slowly over backwards until he was skating on his hands and feet again, leading now with his feet, his belly curved and facing up to the sky.

He stopped, was perfectly still for a second, then began to skate in the opposite direction. He completed a circle around the lamppost, then slowly began to bring his upper body up until he was erect again and skating backwards.

It was a spectacular display. I began to applaud wildly. I pulled Peggy closer to the edge of the circle of light in which the skaters were performing and we watched them. They seemed engrossed in their performance and unaware of us. But when, after a while, we began to move away, they followed.

Peggy said, "Isn't that nice?"

"They're serenading us," I said.

Perhaps because he had seen my costume beneath my open overcoat, the skater who was dressed like me broke away from the group and began to circle about us. Peggy and I clapped our hands and smiled to encourage him. He circled us slowly two or three times, then stretched out a gloved hand, palm up, as if for me to hit it. I hit it eagerly.

I wanted to express my appreciation for his performance. I felt a slight electric shock and pulled my hand quickly out of his, laughing at the prank. He threw his head backwards, uttered no sound, But I imagined that, behind his mask, he was laughing, too.

He offered me his hand again. I took it, prepared to be shocked. I felt nothing. I laughed. He circled a few times, then offered his hand. I took it, uncertain whether I would be shocked or not. After he had done this three or four times, I began to enjoy playing with him. I found the game pleasantly confusing.

His companions were skating ahead of us. Every now and then they fanned out and disappeared into the dimly lit night, like scouts reconnoitring or like babies testing how far they could move away from their parents before returning to them. From time to time, they fell back and joined their friend in skating around us. It was, indeed, as if they were, with their performance, serenading Peggy and me.

We were now on the other side of the theatre. Half the width of the plaza away, the flashing lights of cars and other traffic marked the street on the edge of the neighbourhood where Paul lived. The plaza was darker. The skater offered me his hand. I took it, in the spirit of our game, and this time, the force of the electric shock almost lifted me off the ground.

Even as I felt that unexpected jolt I heard Peggy scream. Dazed, I turned and saw her struggling, no longer screaming, a gloved hand over her mouth. I started towards her and, out of the corner of an eye, saw a hand-held skate coming towards the side of my head. I fell to the ground, and caught a glimpse of a skated foot just before my head seemed to explode. I did not see the next blow. The world seemed to have fallen about my head and to have annihilated me.

★

One night, much, much later, on my bed in my single room in the hospital, I felt suddenly that I was alive again. I remembered Peggy telling me that her book had won the National Book Award. I saw clearly that she was not crying as she told me so. Every memory from the jumbled, unfocused period that preceded this moment of lucidity was suddenly clear and ordered and logical again. Each memory was separate and I did not confuse one with another. I saw Peggy crying and knew that it was because she was telling me she could not honourably marry me, not after what had happened. And I knew she had told me this after she told me that her father was dead. I could figure now that she must have thought that the news of her father's death would give me something to want to live for. I heard Selwyn tell me again, this time clearly and without background noise of any kind in my head, as I forced myself to listen to what he said, that I was very lucky to be alive. Lying alone now in my bed, I contradicted him as I had wanted to then, but had felt too tired at the time to do so.

My head began to ache. I put off calling the nurse as she had instructed me to do. I remembered Frederick. It was his death that had screamed out at me from the papers when Peggy and I were walking home after the party. Paul, wanting to encourage me to fight for my life, had stressed how much Frederick had fought for his. When they found his body next to his wallet, empty except for the pictures he had shown us, and next to the split tire he had stopped to change, his clothes were torn and there were bits of flesh and clotted blood beneath his fingernails.

I wanted them killed, those murderers, whoever they were. And I wanted killed, too, those who had abandoned them like dogs to become wild and dangerous. And it all seemed so absurd that I began to cry.

The nurse came in. She wanted to comfort and encourage me. She told me I shouldn't cry and reminded me of how much progress I had made. She said that I should celebrate instead. I was out of danger now. She told me I was safe.

I didn't contradict her.

ABOUT THE AUTHOR

Garth St Omer was born in Castries, St Lucia in 1931. During the earlier 1950s, he was part of a group of artists in St Lucia including Roderick and Derek Walcott and the artist Dunstan St Omer. In 1956 he went to study French and Spanish at UWI in Jamaica. During the 1960s he travelled widely, including years spent teaching in Ghana. His first publication, the novella, *Syrop*, appeared in 1964, followed by *A Room on the Hill* (1968), *Shades of Grey* (1968), *Nor Any Country* (1969) and *J—, Black Bam and the Masqueraders* in 1972. In the 1970s he moved to the USA, where he completed a doctoral thesis at Princeton University in 1975. Until his retirement as Emeritus Professor, he taught at the University of Santa Barbara in California. The writing of *Prisnms* (Prisons/Prisms) began at some point in the mid 1970s, went through a number of substantial structural revisions in the 1980s, to take the form it is currently published in by c. 1990, though Garth St Omer's continuing engagement with the novel is shown by his making of a significant number of textual revisions after the novel was accepted by Peepal Tree in 2014.

ALSO BY GARTH ST OMER

A Room on the Hill
ISBN: 9781845230937; pp. 162; pub. 2012; price: £8.99

A Room on the Hill is a devastating portrayal of an island
society (much resembling St Lucia in the early 1950s)
suffocating in its smallness, its colonial hierarchies of race
and class and firmly in the grip of a then reactionary
Catholic church – which insisted, for instance, on different
school uniforms for the children of the married and unmar-
ried, and three grades of funeral. The novel focuses on a
small circle of the educated middle class, whose response to
colonial society ranges from acquiescence, finding cynical
self-advantage in the new anti-colonial politics, suicidal
despair and various shades of rebellion. Its astringent real-
ism in questioning the direction of West Indian nationhood
is finely balanced by metaphors of as yet untapped potential.

At the heart of the novel are two characters, John Lestrade,
who feels trapped between his desire to lead an authentic
life and his despair that this may be impossible on his island,
and Anne-Marie D'aubain, who unremarked by the other
characters, shows the possibility of a courageous existential
revolt against the absurdity of circumstance.

First published in 1968, St Omer's novel is distinguished
by its sensitivity to issues of gender, its elegant concision
and, in its existential questioning, its intensive focus on the
inner person. If the world it describes has gone, *A Room on
the Hill* lives on as a major attempt to bring modernity to the
aesthetics of the Caribbean novel.

Shades of Grey
ISBN: 9781845230920; pp. 194; pub. 2013; price: £8.99

As Stephenson comes closer to his girlfriend Thea, with her easy talk of three generations in her family, he has to acknowledge that his past is a blank. He has never known his father, not lived with his mother, and cannot remember what his grandparents looked like. He knows, too, that his failure to come clean about a disreputable episode in his life threatens their relationship. *The Lights on the Hill*, the first of two interdependent short novels in *Shades of Grey*, is a moving and inward portrait of a man, blown along by circumstance, trying in his halting way to construct his own story.

Another Place, Another Time goes back to the character of Derek Charles, who appears as a returning islander in St Omer's first novel, *A Room on the Hill*. Here, almost a decade earlier, St Omer explores the circumstances in which the scholarship boy makes the decision to separate himself from his family and friends and conclude that "He had no cause nor any country now other than himself." As in all St Omer's fiction, there is a sharp focus on the inequalities of gender, and a compassionate but unwavering judgement of the failings of his male characters.

Nor Any Country
ISBN: 9781845232291; pp. 126; pub. 2013; price: £8.99

Education has taken Peter Breville away from his native St Lucia for the past eight years. Now, appointed to a university post in Jamaica, he decides he must see his family on his way from England. There is his mother, whom he loves, his father with whom he has never got on, and his brother, with whom boyhood competition turned sour. And there is Phyllis, his wife, who, though he has not once contacted her since he left, has waited patiently for his return, determined to be a wife to him. Once a desirable catch for a black boy because of her light brownness, Phyllis is now divided from Peter through his access to education and metropolitan experience.

In the week he spends with his family and meeting old friends, he discovers a St Lucia that, in the early 1960s, is on the point of emerging into the modern capitalist world, but where the disparities between the new middle class and the impoverished black majority has become ever wider. In the midst of this, he must decide what he owes Phyllis.

Nor Any Country, first published in 1968, is a profound and elegantly written exploration of the complexities of individual moral choice and an acutely insightful study of a society in the process of change.

J—, Black Bam and the Masqueraders
ISBN: 9781845232436; pp. 128; pub. 2015; price: £8.99

This is the final instalment in a quartet of novels that explores the lives of the small St Lucian middle class in the 1960s. In it the reader re-encounters the brothers, Peter and Paul Breville. Peter, after years abroad, has resumed his marriage with his long abandoned wife Phyllis (the subject of *Nor Any Country*), and is now working as a lecturer in Jamaica. His brother Paul remains in St Lucia, disgraced and sacked from professional employment in a society still dominated by a censorious Catholic church, by his refusal to marry his pregnant girlfriend. He has acquired a reputation for madness, though whether this is a contrived mask or an actual breakdown is left uncertain.

J—, Black Bam and the Masqueraders intercuts Paul's confessional letters to Peter about his destructive relationship with the girl he abandons with the narrative of Peter's marital relationship with Phyllis, his affairs and descent into despair, drunkenness and domestic violence. In the contrast between Paul's self-lacerating honesty and Peter's self-deceptions, St Omer offers a bracingly bleak portrayal of a middle class beset with hypocrisies over race, sexism and class privilege. If sanity is at some level marked by truthful perceptions, St Omer invites us to question which of the brothers is actually sane. It is also a novel where St Omer portrays a black woman quite literally fighting back.

There is no Caribbean novelist who exposes the realities behind the masks people wear or the gaps between postcolonial rhetoric and the actuality of minds that remain deeply colonised with greater economy or elegance. Though first published in 1972, St Omer's novel has lost none of its uncomfortable truth-telling power.

PEEPAL TREE

www.peepaltreepress.com

Peepal Tree Press is the world's leading publisher of Caribbean and Black British writing. Established in 1986, we publish around 20 titles a year and have well over 300 books in print, including many prize-winning titles, the acclaimed Caribbean Modern Classics series, and many exciting new voices.

Peepal Tree Press titles are available from good booksellers all around the world, and direct from our website, where you'll discover all our titles, a wealth of author information, free e-books and much more.

Peepal Tree Press Ltd.
Registered Office 17 King's Avenue, Leeds LS6 1QS, United Kingdom
Telephone +44 (0)113 2451703
www.peepaltreepress.com

Trade Distribution & Representation
UK: Inpress www.inpressbooks.co.uk USA: IPG www.ipgbook.com
Caribbean: orders@peepaltreepress.com

Read our newsletters!

facebook /peepaltreepress

twitter @peepaltreepress